BAD MOON OVER
DEVIL'S RIDGE

Sheriff Cassidy Yates rides into Eagle Heights only to land in jail on an unfounded murder charge. Although Cassidy answers the charge, his wayward brother becomes implicated in the murder and the kidnapping of the dead man's widow. In a town gripped by a conspiracy of fear, Cassidy is helped by a newspaper correspondent to find the real killer and the kidnapped woman. But gun-toting ranchers and hired guns stand between Cassidy and justice — can he prove his brother's innocence?

Books by I. J Parnham
in the Linford Western Library:

THE OUTLAWED DEPUTY
THE LAST RIDER FROM HELL
BAD DAY IN DIRTWOOD
DEVINE'S LAW
YATES'S DILEMMA
DEAD BY SUNDOWN
CALHOUN'S BOUNTY
CALLOWAY'S CROSSING

I. J. PARNHAM

◆

BAD MOON OVER DEVIL'S RIDGE

Complete and Unabridged

LINFORD
Leicester

First published in Great Britain in 2006 by
Robert Hale Limited
London

First Linford Edition
published 2008
by arrangement with
Robert Hale Limited
London

British Library CIP Data

Parnham, I. J.
    Bad moon over Devil's Ridge.—
    Large print ed.—
    Linford western library
    1. Western stories
    2. Large type books
    I. Title
    823.9′2 [F]

    ISBN 978–1–84782–092–1

Published by
F. A. Thorpe (Publishing)
Anstey, Leicestershire

Set by Words & Graphics Ltd.
Anstey, Leicestershire
Printed and bound in Great Britain by
T. J. International Ltd., Padstow, Cornwall

This book is printed on acid-free paper

1

'Reach or die!'

Nick Kearney thrust his hands above his head. Then, as Luther Manson roughly frisked him, he turned away to avoid the bandit's ripe smell. He had nothing that Luther would consider valuable on him, except for the one possession he personally valued and it wasn't long before Luther clasped a dirty hand into Nick's jacket and located it.

'That's nothing you want,' Nick said, managing to keep the tremor in his voice under control but instantly regretting saying the one thing that would interest this notorious bandit.

'Oh?' Luther said, his cruel eyes gleaming as he withdrew the ornate pen. He glared at it as if he'd never seen such a thing before, then even sniffed it before he shrugged and dropped it to the floor. Then he grabbed Nick's arm and threw him towards the side of the car to join Jackson Dyer, the conductor.

As Luther swaggered away, Nick lowered his head to avoid looking at the discarded pen. Even a glance might result in the bandit grinding it into the floor, and right now he needed that pen more than he'd ever needed it. Besides, Nick knew the routine. During the six months he'd been a train butch on the Kansas Pacific railroad, the train had been raided on three previous occasions. So by now he knew exactly how to avoid drawing attention to himself and so how to keep himself alive.

This time, Luther Manson and his gang of bandits had already divested the passengers of their valuables in the first car and now they were starting work on the second car. Luther had five men with him, each man keeping his face hidden by a kerchief, but the overconfident Luther didn't bother with such protection. Two men were elsewhere on the train, subduing the passengers, and with him in this car were the three other men. These men stood back, waiting for Luther to order them to trawl for valuables.

Nick looked up and watched Luther walk away. He noted his arrogant swagger, the way his men responded to his slightest gesture, the way he grinned, relishing the passengers' fearful anticipation of what a man who didn't bother to disguise his appearance was capable of doing.

Nick smiled. It was details such as these that only an eyewitness would notice and they would add colour to the report he'd write the moment this raid ended.

Two seats from the door Luther stopped walking. He glanced back down the train towards the huddled employees and declined his head slightly, almost as if he was acknowledging someone, then turned to look at a man and woman who were sitting side by side on one of the seats. Both people were dressed smartly, marking them out

3

as providing rich pickings, but then again many of the other people on the train were just as well-dressed and Nick saw no reason for Luther to stop and appraise them. But for long moments he stared down at them.

Neither person looked up and it wasn't until Luther uttered a low, commanding growl that the woman turned. She was sitting by the window and her gaze ran up to consider the snarling bandit.

A scream tore from her lips, the sound echoing in the otherwise silent car. Then the man at her side leapt up, his raised arms jerking down to his jacket as he embarked on a futile effort to reach a concealed gun.

His hand was still moving when two shots hammered into his back from two of Luther's men, the blows stumbling him forward until he folded over the seat before him. The woman screeched, fear rooting her to her seat as the man with grim determination righted himself and staggered round to confront

Luther. And while he'd been leaning over the seat he'd managed to locate his gun. He swung it up, but before he could fire, Luther ripped out his own weapon.

Three crisp shots tore out, slamming the wounded man back into the window and cracking the pane, before a fourth shot tumbled him out through the broken glass to land outside, a dull thud sounding.

The woman leapt to her feet and braved the jagged shards of glass to peer out at the fallen man. But she never got the chance to look as Luther swooped in and gathered her up in his arms.

He uttered a loud cry of triumph then fired up into the roof. 'We ride!' he roared.

His men stood boggling at him and darting their gazes around the remaining passengers in the car, all still in possession of their valuables, but then one of the bandits joined Luther in shooting up into the roof.

'You heard Luther,' he shouted, and with that declaration another burst of jubilant gunfire sounded from elsewhere along the train.

With the woman clasped to his chest Luther backed away down the aisle. She uttered a heart-rending plea for someone to save her before Luther clamped a hand over her mouth, leaving her to convey her desperate fear with only her darting eyes. Then Luther dragged her through the door and out of Nick's view. The bandits trooped out after him and made ready to leave, except for one bandit who stayed back to ensure nobody did anything foolish.

Through the windows, Nick saw men scurrying around as the bandits gained their horses. He caught a last glimpse of the frantic woman. Her arms were wheeling as she battered Luther with her small fists, but her assault had no effect on her captor and in a casual manner he handed her over to one of his men. This man dragged her over the back of his horse before the gang moved out of sight.

The bandit who'd stayed back in the car provided a last menacing glare at the passengers and a grunted warning to avoid coming after them. Then he hurried outside.

With much whooping, the Luther Manson gang galloped away, leaving everyone in the train to slowly organize themselves. Several foolhardy individuals hurried out to face the fleeing bandits and they even loosed off several rounds at their backs, but when Luther's men returned gunfire they soon hightailed it back into the train.

As everyone checked that aside from the dead man everyone had escaped from the terrible situation with their lives intact, albeit with their possessions mainly stolen, Nick sighed with relief and turned to Jackson.

'Do you know who that woman was?' he asked.

'That,' Jackson said, 'was Katherine Glover, the widow of the richest man in Eagle Heights.'

'A kidnapping,' Nick mused, rubbing his chin.

'Yeah, and she sure is having a run of bad luck. She was returning to town for her husband's funeral.'

'Was she really?' Nick couldn't help but let a smile break out.

Jackson considered that smile, his flared eyes irritated and accusing.

'What in tarnation have you found in that sorry tale to smile about?'

'We're only five miles out of Eagle Heights,' Nick said, somewhat abashed. He dropped to his knees to reclaim his pen, then jumped to his feet with it brandished aloft. 'And I've just got myself my first ever story for the Eagle Heights *Chronicle*.'

*   *   *

Weaver Dale had just made his second big mistake and Sheriff Cassidy Yates would make him pay for it.

Cassidy had been on Weaver's trail for the last three weeks. He'd been chasing Luther Manson's bandit gang ever since they'd raided Monotony's bank, and so far his only lead had been Weaver, a known outlaw who had probably joined Luther for that one raid, then left.

Cassidy had pursued him to within twenty miles of Eagle Heights, but then his quarry had holed up in the sprawling expanse of caves and blind gulches known as Devil's Ridge, aiming to lie low until Cassidy moved on. But Cassidy wasn't the sort of man who ever gave up and when Weaver had emerged from his bolt-hole he'd followed him. Now he stood before the town's only saloon and Weaver's distinctive roan mare was tethered outside.

Cassidy clumped on to the boardwalk then nudged through the batwings. The main room was heaving and Cassidy quickly slipped into the crowd to search out his quarry. He roved his gaze across the sprawling mass of cowboys who were jostling for position before the bar, then around the raucous gaming-tables until his gaze centred on the faro table.

Weaver was sitting there, his back to the door — a third and final mistake.

Cassidy paced across the room, rounding several tables to approach him. He got to within five paces of him when the dealer murmured a few low words to Weaver. It was unlikely to have been a comment about who was approaching, but Weaver immediately leapt to his feet and swirled round.

For a frozen moment they locked gazes — Cassidy's was calm, Weaver's was wide-eyed and shocked — but one of the many customers in the saloon happened to wander by and Weaver took advantage of his luck. He grabbed the man's shoulder, halting him, then shoved him towards Cassidy. The man stumbled into Cassidy, then grabbed hold of him to stop himself falling. With this man being too drunk to realize who had shoved him Cassidy wasted valuable seconds extricating himself.

When he'd dragged himself clear, Weaver had already slipped from his view and he had to swirl round on the spot, searching for him. Again, he lost valuable moments before his gaze alighted on the man running for the door, barging people aside in his haste to get outside.

Three weeks ago Weaver had shot the only person to die in the Monotony bank raid in cold blood, so Cassidy had no qualms about gunning down this low-life. But as he didn't dare shoot at him in a crowded saloon, he broke into a run and followed.

Weaver clattered through the batwings then hurtled down the boardwalk, running away from his roan.

Cassidy was ten paces behind him as he reached the door then side-stepped through the batwings when they swung out to their utmost. He swirled round and was just in time to see Weaver disappear into Arthur McIntyre's mercantile. Cassidy ran after him, sprinting the few yards past the saloon to the store, then drew his gun and charged in through the door. He leapt to the side, keeping low to stand crouched by the wall in case Weaver was waiting for him to come in. But Weaver wasn't in sight and neither was anyone else.

Cassidy stood still, running his gaze around the store. Only one other door led out of the room, facing him behind the counter. Stacked boxes, sacks, and barrels created a warren of aisles to Cassidy's right, the lefthand side of the store being relatively open.

The door behind the counter creaked open. Cassidy flicked up his gun as the door swung out to its utmost, but the man who emerged was short, portly and clad in a black apron, presumably this was Arthur, the store owner. Arthur took in the sight of Cassidy holding a gun on him with barely a flicker of concern, then he spoke up.

'What you . . . ?'

Cassidy thrust a finger to his lips, silencing him, then gestured around the store, asking silently if he could see where Weaver was hiding.

He received a quizzical raised eyebrow in response, but Cassidy judged his bemusement as confirmation that Weaver hadn't slipped out through the door. That meant he was in this room somewhere and so Cassidy pushed himself slowly away from the wall.

He paced towards the first aisle of sacks, then darted a glance down them, but Weaver wasn't there. Then he headed to the second and again risked darting his gaze down the aisle. Weaver still wasn't there.

He glanced at Arthur who had now understood Cassidy's intent and was rocking from foot to foot and darting his gaze around, but as Cassidy hadn't identified himself as a lawman, he was unsure as to whether he'd help him.

Cassidy had three more aisles to search and he slipped closer to the next. He was just preparing himself to dart forward when a shadow edged forward. At that precise moment Arthur screeched.

'Watch out!' he yelled.

Cassidy darted back, fearing gunfire, but he wasn't quick enough to avoid a corn-sack that Weaver had pushed off the top of the aisle. It caught him a glancing blow on the shoulder, knocking him back and then to one knee.

Another shadow swept over Cassidy as Weaver leapt down from his hiding-place on the top of the sacks. He landed to Cassidy's side, righted himself with surprising agility, then kicked out, his boot planting itself on Cassidy's chest and bundling him on to his back. Then Weaver ran for the door, yanking it open and hurrying out on to the boardwalk.

Cassidy rolled until he lay flat then slipped up to his knees and feet. Then he ran for the door. Weaver had only a few seconds on him as he dashed outside. But then he had to stop himself dead and snap his head back, narrowly avoiding a slug that whistled by his nose and dug splinters from the door-jamb.

Panicked shouting erupted from outside as Weaver planted another slug

14

in the door, then more shouting as another shot ripped out. As Weaver would have no qualms about shooting innocent bystanders if it'd help him escape, Cassidy had no choice but to follow him out.

Cassidy crouched, then leapt through the door, keeping low. A bullet whined over his tumbling form, only the fact he'd thrown himself straight to the boardwalk saving him. He hit the wood, kept rolling as he slipped off the boardwalk, then dug an elbow in, halting himself, and swung both his arms straight out, aiming down the road.

Several people were out on the road, but his gaze centred in on the man on the side of the boardwalk who was swinging his gun round to follow his tumbling form — Weaver Dale.

Cassidy had just a moment to still himself before firing, but it was enough. His single deadly shot tore into Weaver's chest, throwing him backwards and into a post, where he folded

15

round it before sliding to the ground, leaving behind a red snail's-trail.

Cassidy lay for a moment, ensuring Weaver wouldn't get up, then jumped to his feet and paced down the road. As intrigued people spilled out of the saloon, he gestured with a calming wave of a hand, conveying that the crisis was over. Arthur joined Cassidy in standing over the body of Weaver.

'Who was he?' he asked.

'Name's Weaver Dale,' Cassidy said, 'wanted for murder in Monotony.'

'Then it seems he got the justice he deserved.'

'As will the rest of the bandits he was with,' Cassidy said, reaffirming the promise he'd made three weeks ago.

'And who are you?'

'I'm Cassidy Yates, sheriff of Monotony.'

Arthur nodded, his eyes flickering with something, perhaps alarm, but before Cassidy could ask what the problem was, a grunted order to turn round sounded behind him. He turned to face a man with a star, the sheriff of

Eagle Heights, two surly deputies flanking him.

'So,' Sheriff McGill said, standing casually with one leg thrust forward and his hand drifting close to his holster, 'you're Cassidy Yates.'

'Sure am,' Cassidy said, holstering his gun, 'and if you don't know about Weaver Dale, I'll be pleased to fill you in on all the details.'

'Oh, I know all about Weaver Dale.' McGill smiled, but then replaced his jovial expression with a cold-eyed glare. 'But the only question on my mind is about you and what you've done.'

Cassidy gestured around him at the numerous onlookers.

'I reckon I've got a whole heap of witnesses here who saw that Weaver gave me no choice but to shoot him.'

'I'm sure that's right, but I don't mean what you did today, I mean what you did last week.'

'Last week I was holed up on Devil's Ridge, staking this one out.'

'If that's your story, you won't find

many people who'll believe it, and that includes me.' McGill gestured right then left and his two deputies drew their guns, aiming them squarely at Cassidy's chest. 'Cassidy Yates, I'm arresting you for murder, rape, and horse-thieving. Come quietly or die where you stand.'

2

Nick Kearney ran as fast he could along the boardwalk, his breath wheezing, his aching legs protesting, but he now had just another hundred yards to run before he reached the newspaper office.

Luther Manson had raided the train five miles out of Eagle Heights, and as soon as the bandit had gone two men had ridden into town to get help while the railroad staff comforted the passengers. Nick had helped at first but it wasn't long before the pressing need to write down a full report of the incident he'd witnessed defeated his desire to help and he'd slipped out of the train.

Sitting beside the tracks, looking down towards the long blue snake of the river that arced around Eagle Heights, he'd written down the facts of the raid using the required matter-of-fact manner. Then, with the engineer confirming that the raid had damaged and derailed one car, which along with the barrier on the tracks meant this train wouldn't head into town for several days, he'd set off for town on foot.

He'd never tried to run for this sort of distance before and soon his initial burst of speed had petered out and he'd slowed to a combination of fast walking and short frantic bursts of running. By the time he'd reached Eagle Heights he was sweating profusely and muscles he didn't know he had were protesting.

He consoled himself with the thought that it'd all be worth his pains in a few minutes. So with a gut-churning mixture of fevered anticipation and desperate hope, he stomped to a halt outside the office of the Eagle Heights *Chronicle*. He gathered his breath then pushed open the door.

Inside, Henry Sinclair, the editor, was hunched over a huge slab of machinery. At his feet was a pile of paper, and as he didn't look up Nick got to say the words he'd dreamed of saying for the last six months.

'Stop that press!' he shouted, then bent himself double to wheeze his breath in and out of his cramped lungs.

Henry leaned back to look at him.

'And who wants me to do such a damn fool thing?' he said, acknowledging him with a curt nod.

'Nick, Nick Kearney,' Nick managed to say between gasps. He watched Henry narrow his eyes and waited for him to recognize him, but when several embarrassing seconds had passed without Henry showing any sign of working out who he was, he explained. 'I came to you six months ago, looking for a job with your newspaper. You said you couldn't take me on, but you said if I ever came across a story for the *Chronicle*, you'd reconsider. And now, I've got me that story.'

Henry waved with a dismissive gesture towards the door.

'Then come back later and tell me all about it. I'm too busy right now. I've got a special issue to get out.'

Henry pointed to the huge pile of paper on the floor, then moved to bend over his equipment again, but Nick stopped him with a loud demand.

'But you'll want to add my report to your special issue. This is a story everyone will want to read about.'

Henry straightened his back slowly and faced Nick.

'Then don't keep me waiting. What you got?'

'Luther Manson raided the train bound for Eagle Heights and — '

'And he kidnapped James Glover's widow.'

The room appeared to lurch and Nick had to close his eyes for a moment to overcome the sudden burst of nausea that threatened to overwhelm him.

'How . . . How did you get to know about that so soon?'

'I'm a newspaper man,' Henry said, his simple declaration stated with a mixture of assurance and pride. He peeled off the topmost sheet from the pile at his feet and held it out.

Nick took the single sheet and turned it round to read.

'James Glover's widow abducted,' he said, reading the headline, 'by Luther Manson's bandit gang.'

He scanned down the remainder of the sheet, discovering that the entire tale he had planned to sell to Henry was there, plus some details he had missed.

'You got anything to add or can I carry on printing?' Henry asked. 'News is only news while someone will pay to read it, and I just haven't got the time to waste.'

'No,' Nick murmured, crestfallen. 'You got the whole story I had to sell down here.'

Henry nodded, leaving Nick to slump his shoulders and contemplate the most disappointing failure he'd suffered so far during his short career as a potential journalist. But the irrepressible attitude that had motivated him through the last six months defeated his sudden burst of depression and he hurried to Henry's side.

'I may not have got that story to you first, Mr Sinclair, but it still is the right story, so do you want to reconsider your offer? I reckon I've proved I'll make a fine correspondent.'

Henry shrugged. 'Haven't got the time to teach you to be a newspaper man right now, but I'll give you one piece of advice if you ever want me to reconsider.' Henry waggled a reproachful finger at Nick. 'Being second with a story is worse than having no story at all. Next time, remember that before you come to me with something to sell.'

Nick winced, but then ran Henry's comment through his mind and decided that he might not have succeeded this time, but Henry was saying if he succeeded next time, he would consider him.

'Mr Sinclair,' he declared, 'I'll remember that advice and I'm obliged to you for giving it to me.'

He made to turn to the door, but

Henry stopped him by nodding towards the pile of printed special issues.

'And I'll give you one more piece of advice. Take a copy — for no charge — and read it thoroughly from top to bottom.' Henry winked with what Nick took to be a friendly and encouraging gesture. 'Maybe it'll help you work out how you could get to be that newspaper man one day.'

★　★　★

'Why have you locked me in here?' Cassidy Yates demanded, slapping the bars. 'Because I sure don't know nothing about those charges.'

Sheriff McGill considered Cassidy through the bars with his arms folded and a sneer on his lips. His deputies flanked him, all showing just as much contempt with their surly gazes.

'I'll explain,' McGill said, 'when *I* choose to do so.'

Cassidy lowered his voice to a more conciliatory tone.

25

'I overheard you talking about Luther Manson raiding the train. I've been on his tail for three weeks after he raided the bank in Monotony. The longer you keep me in here, the further he'll get away from us.'

'There is no us. There's just . . . ' The door to the sheriff's office creaked open and McGill flicked his gaze to the new arrival, a smartly dressed businessman, then frowned and turned back to Cassidy. 'There's just me and my deputies and we'll be the ones who'll track him down. All you'll do is sit quietly and await justice.'

As the deputies grunted their approval, Cassidy slumped down on to his cot and watched McGill turn away to face the newcomer.

'Why in tarnation,' the newcomer demanded, pacing up to the sheriff to loom over him, 'are you still here?'

'I'm sorry, Tex,' McGill said, then pointed to the cells. 'But I arrested this man and — '

'Is he one of Manson's men?'

In his cell, Cassidy met the flared gaze of a man who from McGill's comment he now identified as being Tex Beatty, one of the wealthiest men in Eagle Heights.

'No,' McGill said. 'I want this one for something else. It's Sheriff Cassidy Yates.'

Tex sneered. 'Oh, that one. There's nothing I hate more than a lawman who's gone bad.'

'Hey,' Cassidy shouted, jumping to his feet, 'I don't even know why you're holding me.'

Tex and McGill looked his way to appraise him then turned their backs on him with studied disdain and finality.

'Do you reckon,' Tex said, drawing McGill away towards the door, 'that Bret Sanborn is right and he killed James?'

McGill shrugged. 'I haven't had the time to question him yet.'

'In that case,' Tex muttered, his lowering of tone seeming to dismiss the issue of Cassidy from his thoughts, 'what are you doing to find Katherine?'

'I'm leaving right now.'

Tex raised his heels as well as his voice to loom further over McGill and browbeat him.

'Then quit wasting time talking to me and get out there.'

McGill didn't balk at Tex's inappropriate orders and he acknowledged his duty with a nod. He gestured to one of his deputies, Deputy Lomax, to stay in the office, then headed out with the other one, Kendrick, leaving Tex to walk to the cell to consider Cassidy.

'You delayed Sheriff McGill,' he muttered, 'when he should have been looking for Katherine. I'll make you pay for that.'

'I don't know the details of what's happened to this woman,' Cassidy said, 'but the moment I get out of here I will help — '

'You will never get out of there. James ain't around no more, but I'm sure he'd say you never seek the help of someone like you. I'd sooner she die than have her live because of your help.'

With that pronouncement, Tex turned on his heel and left Cassidy alone with Deputy Lomax.

This man considered Cassidy with what Cassidy was starting to view as his permanent surly expression, then sauntered a few paces closer to the cells. He rolled his tongue around his lips, chewing, before he launched a great gob of spit at the base of the cell bars.

'What you probably didn't realize,' he drawled, 'is that James was Tex's business partner. Since James got himself all shot to pieces last week Tex's been mighty touchy. Now Katherine's kidnapping has sure hit him bad.'

'And like I said, once this is over, I'll help you find the man who shot him.'

Cassidy smiled, hoping he could foster some common understanding with his jailer, but Lomax sneered, suggesting he already thought Cassidy was guilty.

'Ain't no need for no finding now.'

'Lomax, I'm a lawman like you. I'm

innocent of all these crimes, but I respect justice, so don't go overstepping yourself with that attitude until the full facts come out and I receive proper justice.'

Lomax snorted, then headed to the door. He slipped his head outside to look up and down the road, then clicked his fingers and slipped back in.

'I guess we're about to find out,' he said, pausing to lick his lips with obvious relish, 'just how much you crave that justice.'

'I don't know what you . . . ' Cassidy trailed off as the men to whom Lomax had gestured outside paced into the sheriff's office.

There were three of them, all hard-boned and cold-eyed. They lined up before the cell, considering Cassidy while cracking knuckles or flexing their fists.

Lomax drew his gun and held it on Cassidy, then ordered one of the men, Chalk, to fetch the key to Cassidy's cell. Chalk unlocked and swung open the cell door. Then the men filed into the cell. Cassidy didn't think it was worth trying to talk them round from doing what they had clearly planned to do the moment McGill left. So Cassidy slowly backed away, ensuring he kept the wall at his back and so limiting the directions from which they could attack him.

There was barely enough room to accommodate all four men in the cell; in such a confined space the restrictions might even help him, but only if he had some luck.

One man stepped forward and swung a punch at Cassidy's head. Cassidy easily ducked under it and came up, moving forward. He barged into the man and knocked him back, even getting that luck he'd hoped for as the man stumbled into one of his other assailants and brought him down.

As these two men floundered, Cassidy swung round to face Chalk. He weaved away from a scything punch, then followed through with a flurry of blows to face and chest that tipped Chalk out through the open door to land sprawled on his chest.

'Don't think much of your justice,' Cassidy said, enjoying his moment of success as he looked down at the three felled men.

'We've only just started on you,' Lomax said with a barely suppressed chuckle. 'And you've just gone and got them all angry.'

The two men in the cell extricated themselves and when they came to their feet they moved in cautiously, coming at him at the same time from two different directions and darting glances at each other to coordinate their actions. Cassidy didn't give them the chance to make their move and charged the first man with his arms outstretched. He slapped his arms around the man's chest and carried him back into the cell bars, pinning him there, then reached up and grabbed his chin, slamming his head back into the bars.

The man struggled, trying to free

himself but Cassidy slammed his head back a second time, trying to knock him out. He didn't get the chance when another man leapt on his back. Fingers gouged at his eyes, but Cassidy squirmed and his assailant only managed to cram several fingers into his mouth, a mistake he instantly regretted when Cassidy clamped his jaw closed.

Blood oozed, the taste sharp on Cassidy's tongue, and a pained grunt sounded. Cassidy snarled for added effect as he shook his head back and forth making the man pay for his action. But then a solid blow hammered into the back of his head, knocking the hand away and stumbling him to his knees.

Cassidy just had time to realize that Chalk had come into the cell and had clubbed him over the back of the head when a swinging kick to the guts lifted him off the floor. A second kick sent him rolling into the bars. He lay on his side, looking up to see that his initial success had earned him three men, one bloodied, and all with bloodlust and a determination to make him suffer burning in their eyes.

Cassidy decided not to give them that chance. He slowly got to his knees, feigning being more winded than he was, then to his feet, standing stooped with his arms dangling slackly.

His act fooled nobody as his assailants moved in as one. So Cassidy snapped himself upright. He got in one blow at the nearest man, but then they were on him. Chalk grabbed his arms then swung him round to hold him upright while the others lined up to administer a pummelling.

Cassidy's head rocked one way then the other, the blows jarring even though he rolled as much as he could with them. But after just two blows, Lomax entered the cell with a sack and dragged it down over Cassidy's head, the friction from the rough cloth burning his cheeks.

Then with his vision curtailed Cassidy couldn't tell where the next blow was coming from as they slammed into him with brutal force. Two stinging punches slapped into his guts before one crunched into his face, tearing him away from Chalk and spinning him to his knees.

On all fours he knelt, looking towards the floor he couldn't see. Then a solid kick to his side rolled him away, but not for long as he hit the bars, his head hammering into them with a solid and dull clang.

Merciful oblivion started to steal consciousness away from him as he lay on the floor, but he was aware of the men standing over him and he heard Deputy Lomax speak up.

'Now,' he said, 'let's get him out of here and give him that justice he deserves.'

3

Nick sat on the edge of the boardwalk. On the ground between his feet was the special issue of the Eagle Heights *Chronicle*. He'd done as Henry had advised and read it from top to bottom several times. Also at his feet was his own version of the events.

What he'd read had depressed him even more about his chances of succeeding in his chosen career. He'd missed out many details, such as the reprising of Luther's exploits before the train raid, and many of the details Nick had related he now saw as being too trivial for a newspaper.

Across the road a lamp burned in the office of the Eagle Heights *Chronicle*. Nick couldn't help but let his gaze linger on it, imagining what it'd be like to spend night after night sitting in there, bringing together and reporting on a town's important information. Tonight, that life felt even further away than usual.

The train wouldn't be able to resume its journey for two days and although today's stage could have carried some of the passengers to their destination, everyone had stayed in town. Many were taking solace in the saloon. Nick had yet to develop a taste for liquor but, with his black mood showing no sign of lifting, he was considering developing that taste soon.

Other towns were along the railroad with other newspapers where he might find work, but Henry Sinclair was the only person who had ever encouraged him. So the Eagle Heights *Chronicle* was still his chosen place of work. Now he wished with every fibre of his being that he could have been the one who had got the story to Henry first.

Earlier, Nick had overheard some people talking about a renegade lawman who, amongst other crimes, had killed James Glover last week. This intrigued

Nick and he listened with interest, hoping it might suggest another sellable news item before he had to move on. But he soon lost interest when he learned that the lawman had now been arrested.

Presently, Sheriff McGill and Deputy Kendrick returned to town. Nick stood and took a meandering route across the road, ensuring that when he passed them he was close enough to overhear their conversation and so perhaps learn some useful details of their pursuit of Luther Manson. And he had some luck when Tex Beatty emerged from the saloon and questioned McGill in a loud and belligerent tone.

McGill reported that he'd had no luck in finding Luther's trail, but he promised to start again at first light and not to return until he did find him. Tex grumbled aplenty but with neither man mentioning any interesting facts, Nick couldn't help but search out those trivial details he always noticed. Tex was every bit a dandy dresser and his colourful clothing was perhaps inappropriate when his business partner and friend had just been murdered. Curiously, the same could have been said about James's widow. She hadn't been clad in black and at the time Nick hadn't even considered she was a woman in mourning.

Nick stopped dead in the road, an excited murmur slipping from his lips that stopped both men from exchanging comments to look to him. He acknowledged them with a nod, then turned on his heel and hurried to the newspaper office, his mind whirling with the thought that had just hit him. He ought to think it through, perhaps by writing it down, but this time he reckoned it'd be better to get Henry's advice first.

He opened the door to find Henry wasn't doing what Nick had expected and ruminating on important items of news. He was leaning back in his chair, a foot resting on the top of his desk, a glass in hand and a bottle of whiskey at his side. He hailed Nick with a jovial wave that sloshed whiskey on the floor, then beckoned him to approach.

'Nick Kearney, I do declare,' he said, his cheeks glowing with good humour and liquor. 'See, I remembered you and that's half the battle in becoming a correspondent.'

'Obliged you think I can become one, one day.'

'You can, you can, my boy. You're young enough to have plenty of time to learn the trade.' He raised his eyebrows.

'I'm nineteen come the fall,' Nick said, adding on two years.

Henry considered this information with a narrowing of his eyes.

'Waiting to become a correspondent must be a tiring job if it ages you three years in six months.' Henry sighed and smiled again. 'But even though six months isn't a great length of time, I tell you, young Nick, newspapers have changed a lot since you first poked your head into my office.' Henry drew Nick's attention to the machine that dominated the office. 'Once it used to take me longer to print the paper than write it, but since Ottmar Mergenthaler, glorious man that he is, started selling these here linotype machines, people are paying to read the news faster than it happens.'

Nick looked at the machine that had so pleased Henry. He had never seen its like. It had parts sticking out everywhere and Nick could only guess at their use, although he had once seen something a lot smaller called a typewriter and he guessed the principle might be the same.

'Linotype? Why call it that?'

'Short for line of type, and that's what it does, creates lines and lines of type faster than you and I can read it.' Henry kicked back a chair then gestured towards a glass that was sitting on a heap of papers. 'Well, perhaps not that quickly, but since I bought this, everything's changed.'

Although Nick had yet to appreciate

the appeal of liquor, he did understand its social benefits. He went to the paper pile, seeing that it was this week's normal issue of the Eagle Heights *Chronicle*, now almost complete and ready to sell. He took the glass and poured himself a small measure, then sat.

'I'm just looking for a chance, Mr Sinclair, in this exciting new world. And I've read your special issue and — '

'And you didn't like it.' Henry waited while Nick shook his head and blurted out a denial, then smiled. 'Don't deny it. I can see it in your eyes. But my report was journalism and what you want to write is . . . Well, I reckon it's more akin to those dime-novels you so enjoy reading.'

'Perhaps,' Nick murmured, feeling his cheeks warm as Henry somehow deduced his viewpoint. As a train butch he sold both newspapers and books with lurid covers to the passengers, but he'd read almost as many of those books as he'd sold.

'Then I've got some more advice for you,' Henry declared, pausing to knock back then refill his glass. 'Stop reading that nonsense and read every newspaper you can lay your hands on instead.'

'But I do, I do,' Nick said, feeling aggrieved out of all proportion to Henry's mild admonishment. 'It's just that . . .'

'Go on. The truth never hurts.'

'I reckon . . .' Nick searched for the right words, then gulped his drink and emboldened by the fire burning down his throat, blurted out his complaint. 'I reckon the newspapers could do with more colour. The reports are so dull and so . . .'

'So popular, they sell.' Henry waited for Nick to respond, but Nick could find nothing to say to this and he just fiddled with his empty glass, leaving Henry to lean forward. 'I'll give you another lesson, young Nick. Today, I printed and sold two hundred and sixty seven copies of a single sheet special issue at ten cents a time. Taking off my expenses that's a profit that makes reporting the news worthwhile.'

'Then,' Nick said, brightening as he saw how he could draw the conversation back to his reason for coming here, 'why not print a second special issue tomorrow at another ten cents a time?'

Henry leaned back in his chair. 'Can't do that until more news happens.'

'But it has. Luther Manson is still at large and until he's captured and Katherine Glover is free, everyone will happily pay to read the story of his pursuit and her release.'

'They will, but only if I can get some facts about what's happening.'

'And I have some.'

Henry laughed and slapped his thigh, sloshing whiskey on his leg.

'I thought you had. I had a good feeling about you the first time you walked through that door. I never forget a face and I said to myself, one day this boy will be back with a real story.'

'And here it is.' Nick placed his

empty glass beside the whiskey bottle while he composed his thoughts. 'Tex Beatty dresses in gaudy clothes and so does Katherine Glover.'

Henry spluttered over his whiskey before he replied.

'And that's your story?'

'It's the reason behind the story. Katherine Glover joined the train at Kansas City and throughout the whole journey I didn't even know she was the widow of someone important, nor that she was heading to his funeral.'

Henry shrugged. 'Katherine is a modest and private woman.'

'A woman who isn't as well-known or recognizable as her late husband?'

'She's never sought to be.'

'And I saw that. Most people who consider themselves important can't wait for the train to leave the station before they're telling you who they are and why they should receive special treatment, but not her.'

Henry's eyes flashed with the first glimmer of understanding.

'And you're saying it was mighty odd that Luther Manson should have just happened to kidnap someone who didn't draw attention to who she was?'

'I sure am, and more. The bandits worked their way through one car, taking anything worth stealing, but they didn't steal at all from the second car. Luther just headed to her, grabbed her, and left.'

Henry didn't reply immediately, setting his glass down and rubbing his chin as he thought this through.

'You're saying someone let Luther know who she was?'

'I am, but it's even worse than that. I'm saying the stealing of the valuables in the first car was just to put everyone off the trail because the *only* reason Luther raided the train was to kidnap her.'

'If you're right, that's some mighty fine reasoning.' Henry favoured Nick with a huge smile then replaced it with a deep frown. 'But what I'm not sure about is what story you're trying to sell me.'

'It's a follow-up to today's story. Someone on the train was working for Luther Manson. Katherine must be being held for ransom and someone in this very town probably knows where she is. There's a lawman in jail who killed her husband. And then there's . . . there's . . . ' Nick waved his arms as he tried to put the thoughts that had only just come to him in order. 'There's just got to be a story there.'

As Nick winced at his lame summing-up, Henry shook his head.

'There isn't. What you have is an opinion. You can express an opinion in the company of friends, but aside from a letter to the editor written by yours truly on matters of major importance, there is no room in my newspaper for opinion, just facts.' Henry leaned forward and rested a hand on his knee, placing his face so close to Nick's that Nick's eyes watered from the whiskey fumes. 'Bring me those facts and I might consider your story, until then keep your opinions out of my newspaper office.'

Nick gulped and was about to lower his head in embarrassment for not realizing this, but then saw the encouraging twinkle in Henry's eyes.

'Are you telling me to ... to investigate this myself?'

'I guess I am,' Henry said, patting Nick's knee and giving him his most encouraging smile so far. 'You've got yourself a lead on a sellable story. So sell it to me.'

★　★　★

Lomax and Chalk were moving around nearby, but as Cassidy still had the sack over his head, he didn't know where he'd been brought to, or what they were doing. But he continued to act as if he were unconscious in case an opportunity to escape presented itself.

He'd come to fifteen minutes ago, finding that he was trussed up and slung over the back of a horse, the steady motion and the beating he'd suffered inducing nausea that he'd had to fight down.

But presently, he'd stopped moving. Rough hands had dragged him from the horse. He'd not attempted to keep himself upright.

Accordingly, two men had pulled him to his feet and dragged him along. They had entered a building, Cassidy's trailing feet bouncing up several steps before they'd set him down.

Deputy Lomax had secured him to a chair. Then he'd paid off and dismissed two of the men, leaving just himself and Chalk. From Lomax's echoing tones, the lack of smell, and general airy feel, Cassidy had the impression he was in a substantial room.

More important, he didn't judge that they'd dragged him off to some low shack where they could secretly execute summary justice. So he kept a small glimmer of hope that maybe the justice Lomax had spoken of wouldn't be as bad as it'd sounded.

Presently a door opened. A man entered and paced across the room to stand before him. Through the weave of the sack Cassidy had the impression that he was a large man.

'Admit you're awake, Cassidy,' this man grunted.

Cassidy instantly resolved to stop his attempted subterfuge when it was unlikely to gain him anything. He judged that honesty was the only way he'd get himself out of this situation alive.

'Then tell me who you are and let me see you,' Cassidy said, straightening up. 'Unless you enjoy talking with a man hidden in a sack.'

The man grunted a low command and Lomax dragged the sack from Cassidy's head.

Cassidy blinked hard in response to the sudden brightness, then looked around the room, taking it for being the main room of a ranch house. An unlit fire was beside him and through one window he saw the half-moon hanging in the twilit sky above Devil's Ridge. He returned his gaze to his captor, who loomed over him with Lomax and Chalk flanking him.

'I'm Bret Sanborn,' the man reported, then cocked his head to one side as if he expected Cassidy to recognize the name.

Cassidy recalled that Sheriff McGill and Tex Beatty had spoken about this man, mentioning that he believed Cassidy had killed James Glover. Cassidy chose to keep this knowledge to himself.

'And why have you brought me here, Bret?' he asked.

'If you wish to continue your pretence that you're innocent, do so, but just so we can start, I'll state this: I was a friend of James Glover, the man you killed. My daughter is Annie Sanborn, the woman you raped.' He gestured to the glowering man on his right. 'This man is Chalk Pendleton, the intended of the woman you raped.'

'I am,' Chalk muttered, glaring into

Cassidy's eyes. 'And it was James Glover who was kind enough to lend me the money so that I could get a place all fixed up down by the river for me and Annie to live in once we were wed. Now he's dead, Annie's hurting real bad, and ripping you apart is all I have left to enjoy.'

Cassidy gulped, a curious mixture of relief and trepidation overcoming him. He could well understand now why Lomax and Chalk had bundled him away from his cell and taken him here to receive summary justice. His problem now was to prove to such men that he was innocent.

'You've made a mistake,' he said, speaking slowly. 'I'm an honest lawman, and when you accept that, I'll speak no more about what you've done and help you find the man who really committed those crimes. Then we will deal with him the right way in a court of law.'

Bret flashed a grim smile. 'And the assurance with which you speak those lies shows me how you wormed your way into Annie's trust.'

'I wasn't lying, and although I'd hate to put your daughter through any more stress, we can clear this up easily. Bring her here and let her see me. She'll tell you I'm not that man.'

Bret glanced at Chalk, who glared back at him. Cassidy detected some emotion in their momentary exchange of eye-contact — perhaps doubt.

'If there was any other way,' Bret said, his tone sad, 'I'd take it. So I'll give you this, I don't want Annie to have to face you. Confess now and we'll take you out the back and get this over with real quick.' Bret widened his eyes, his jaw bunching with barely suppressed rage. 'But make me bring her in here and you'll be a long time wishing you'd taken my offer.'

'I can't do that. I know she won't recognize me.'

Bret's gaze again flicked to Chalk, but this time Chalk spoke up. 'He knows something,' he grunted, shaking a bunched fist at Cassidy. 'He knows

Annie won't identify him. He — '

'Enough debate!' Bret shouted, silencing his outburst. 'I have made my offer and Cassidy has refused it. Now we will discover the truth.'

Bret gestured to Chalk, then to the door through which he'd entered earlier, but when Chalk ignored him in favour of continuing to glare at Cassidy, Lomax turned on his heel and headed to the door. Cassidy heard his heels click and echo as he paced down a corridor beyond. Presently, a door opened then closed. The slow footsteps of two people approaching sounded, then stopped. He heard sharp words spoken from beyond the door, some of them were Lomax's and the rest came from a woman.

Cassidy couldn't hear the words but a tense conversation was taking place in which Lomax was urging the woman to do something, presumably come into the room. Accordingly, Cassidy softened his expression to avoid adding to her distress when she faced a man who could be her attacker. By the time she shuffled into the room he was all but smiling.

Annie was young, perhaps eighteen, and slightly built, but deep-set lines marred an oval face, which would otherwise be appealing. Her left hand fingered a shawl, worrying a hole she'd opened through the weaving. She paced across the room without looking up, with Lomax a pace behind her, his jaw set firm as he bored his gaze into Cassidy. Chalk continued to glare at Cassidy, but Bret turned to look at her, offering her a terse but encouraging smile as he held his hand out to stop her coming too close.

She stopped and stared at the floor. A sigh and a low word that Cassidy didn't catch emerged from her lips. Then she slowly looked up to consider him, her eyes wide with what Cassidy took to be an expression akin to hope rather than fear, but then she lowered her head and snuffled.

'That's not him,' she said with

matter-of-fact assurance.

'Take a longer look,' Bret urged as Cassidy exhaled a sigh of relief.

She didn't look up. 'It's just not Cassidy.'

'That man claims to be Sheriff Cassidy Yates,' Bret snapped, raising his voice. 'He even has — '

'I don't know who he is, but he's not *my* Cassidy.'

'Well,' Chalk blurted out, 'she would say that to protect him, wouldn't she? It just proves it is him.'

'It isn't,' she screeched, stamping a foot then swirling round to confront Chalk. 'It isn't. It isn't.'

Bret shook his head, sighing, then gestured for Deputy Lomax to take her away. Lomax placed a hand on her shoulder, but Annie ignored him as she slammed her hands on her hips and confronted Chalk. Even when Lomax took her arm, she shrugged away from his grasp and he had to wrap an arm around her waist and bodily drag her to the door. Still she dug her heels in and uttered one last cry of defiance that they'd got the wrong man before she relented and let Lomax lead her away.

Bret watched her go, muttering to himself, then turned back to Cassidy, who sat straight in his chair.

'She would say that,' Cassidy said, intoning Chalk's words with heavy enunciation, 'to protect him, wouldn't she?'

'This is all very confusing,' Bret said, tipping back his hat to scratch his forehead. He glanced at Chalk, but he was glaring through the door at Lomax's and Annie's receding backs.

'Not to me it isn't,' Cassidy said. 'I can see exactly what's happened here. This man who claimed to be me didn't rape Annie or perhaps even kill James. You're just being over-protective of your — '

'You cannot judge me,' Bret snapped, aiming a firm finger at Cassidy. 'Since Martha died I've run the Devil's Ridge ranch on my own and yet I've still done everything a father could possibly do for his only daughter.'

Cassidy took deep breaths to still his anger and to force himself to concentrate on achieving the most important thing of his own release.

'I can see that,' he said using a soft tone that didn't reflect his feelings. 'Bringing up a daughter on your own must have been tough. You want to protect her, but you can't choose the man she will fall in love with.'

'I sure can.' Bret slapped a firm hand on Chalk's shoulder. 'Chalk is a fine man and the best she could have found.'

Chalk grunted his agreement as Deputy Lomax returned to the room.

'I'm sure he is,' Cassidy said, his low tone betraying his sarcasm, 'but it sounds to me like she chose the best for herself.'

'Cassidy Yates ain't the best for her,' Chalk shouted, pushing past Bret to loom over Cassidy.

Cassidy considered Chalk's bunched fists, then met his angered gaze. 'I'm not, and as that man couldn't tell her the truth about his own name, I reckon you're probably right about him too.'

Chalk acknowledged this fact with a muttered oath. Then in the silent room Deputy Lomax spoke up.

'Untie him,' he said, simply.

Bret looked back to acknowledge his order then gestured to Chalk, who grumbled before he busied himself with releasing Cassidy's bonds.

Lomax paced across the room to stand before him.

'I ain't apologizing for what I did,' he said. 'Justice never seems to come to those who deserve it.' Lomax glared down at Cassidy with steady defiance and when Cassidy didn't reply, he turned to Bret. 'But the worst thing about all of this is that while I was dragging Cassidy out here I was letting down Tex Beatty.'

Bret rocked from foot to foot, staring at the floor and shaking his head. Only when Chalk had freed Cassidy did he turn to him.

'Cassidy, I guess I need to apologize, but you can see why I . . . ' Bret left the rest of his sentiment unsaid.

As Cassidy rubbed his sore wrists and rolled his shoulders, feeling several bruises announce their presence, he didn't feel inclined to forgive him for what he had tried to do. But neither did he feel in the mood nor in the ideal position to lecture Bret on his failings and he limited himself to just standing and turning to the door.

'I'm leaving,' he said.

Cassidy walked a single pace towards the door, but Chalk moved to the side to block his way.

'Don't you go thinking,' he muttered, glaring into Cassidy's eyes, 'you can just walk away from this. I ain't totally convinced you're not her Cassidy. So remember this — I'll be watching you.'

Cassidy felt his anger rise again. 'I sympathise you weren't man enough to keep your woman, but — '

'Say that again,' Chalk roared, stepping up to Cassidy, 'and no matter who you are I'll knock you through that wall.'

'You can try, but as you can't satisfy your — '

'Enough!' Bret snapped, pacing in between the two men and barging them apart. 'Chalk, forget this man and start thinking about our search for the real culprit. Cassidy, don't take your anger out on Chalk.'

Cassidy provided a rueful smile, acknowledging that he had spoken ill-advised words to someone who, given the circumstances, didn't need to hear what he'd just said.

'I guess that was wrong of me,' he offered, lightening his tone, 'but you two have just got to accept that Annie has lost her heart to someone who could well be beneath her. The matter of James's murder is another thing, but I'd let the law decide whether he had anything to do with that.'

'No matter what you say,' Chalk said, 'I won't accept that. We're going after this man and we will — '

Cassidy didn't get to hear the rest of this threat as footsteps pattered down the corridor and the door flew open. Annie hurried in.

'You've all got him wrong,' she shouted, sliding to a halt before the window. 'I don't know who that man is, but my Cassidy is the gentlest and kindest man I've ever met.'

'Then why did he hide from me?' Bret snapped. 'And why did he steal from me? And why did he — ?'

'Because we both knew what you'd say to him. And he took just the one horse to get away from you, and you've got dozens of them. And we all know he didn't kill James Glover.'

Bret didn't respond immediately, savouring the moment before he uttered the one fact she couldn't explain away easily.

'So why did he lie about his name?'

Annie opened her mouth to provide an instant retort, then closed it as she shrugged and fought to find an explanation.

'I'm sure,' she said at last, raising her chin to a dignified height she couldn't feel, 'he had a good reason for doing that and you can ask him what it was when he returns.'

Bret snorted. 'The likes of him will never return now that you've given him what he wanted.'

'He only left because you ran him off, but he will come back, like he promised me.' She turned to the window and looked off into the evening sky. When she spoke again, her voice was wistful and she uttered her words as if she was quoting a favourite piece of poetry. 'Come the new moon, a slim crescent will shine down over Devil's Ridge and I'll be looking to that moon too. And — '

'And maybe not this moon,' Cassidy said, speaking slowly but loudly, his words gradually stopping her from speaking. 'And maybe not the next, but as soon I've got us a place all fixed up, I'll come riding down from Devil's Ridge with the moon at my back. And on that cold, clear night I'll take you with me.'

Annie swirled round to face Cassidy, her mouth falling open in shock.

'How did you know he said that?' she murmured.

Bret stared at Annie and Cassidy in turn, then thrust out an outstretched finger at Cassidy.

'I had just convinced myself,' he blurted out, 'you had nothing to do with this other man who took your name. Then you go and say that. Think long and hard about what you say next because lawman or no lawman I'm minded right now to drag you out the back.'

'There's no need to do that. I know what this man said to Annie because I've heard those words before.' Cassidy paced to Annie's side and looked through the window. In the gathering darkness he could see the moon, red and angry behind low cloud as it headed for the jagged ridge from which no man would ever ride down to her. 'The man who rode off and promised to return one day was Emerson Yates, my brother.'

4

Thirty passengers and six railroad employees had been on the train. In the last three hours Nick had located them all. And every single one of them had looked guilty.

Nick had envisaged his career as a correspondent as being one in which, late at night, he calmly wrote reports on events in the seclusion of the office. He hadn't expected he would have to seek out that information on his own, but after only a few hours of thinking in that way, he was beginning to relish the task. Henry had been right. He had read more dime-novels than newspaper reports, and he'd loved the tales of the Pinkerton detectives. Now he was trying his best to think like one.

Pondering on what he'd learned so far, he left one of Tex's Beatty's two hotels and paced down the road to the saloon. He had just watched a couple book in to a room — innocently, he'd decided. Although in truth their departure to their room had stopped his observing them for any longer.

Someone on the train had identified Katherine Glover to Luther Manson, of this he was certain. Having observed every potential suspect, Nick's thoughts inevitably returned to his prime suspect: Jackson Dyer, Nick's boss and so a man whom he had frequently rubbed up against.

Jackson was always looking for ways to make extra money, before he then gambled that money away, and his schemes were always nefarious. The saying amongst the railroad employees was that anyone who so much as dropped a dime would find Jackson catching it before it hit the floor. So as soon as Nick entered the saloon, he first of all located Jackson.

Right now Jackson was doing what he always did when they stopped over in a town for the night — he was in a poker-game. Except that this time it was a highstakes game.

An appreciative audience had gathered to watch the contest with the usual mixture of interest and ghoulish delight at the possibility of someone being taken for every last cent he had. Jackson was usually one of those hoping to do the taking, but this time Nick couldn't help but think he was the one being primed for the taking.

Jackson sat opposite a Southern gambler, his waxed moustache and gold-embroidered waistcoat being just too obvious a sign of his status to be genuine. A flint-eyed deputy sheriff sat to Jackson's left, watching the others with cold disdain, his cards already thrown to the table.

To Jackson's right sat a furtive and heavily sweating individual, who continually scratched and muttered to himself, then grinned or sobbed into his hands with each card he received.

Nick decided the deputy's disdain was genuine, but the gambler and the sweaty man were both putting on a performance and perhaps were even in league. The trouble for them was, Jackson was experienced enough to know this, neither did he have the funds to make this particular kind of operation worthwhile.

In case he'd misunderstood what was happening, Nick nudged his way through the crowd and took up a close position where he could watch them.

'I reckon this is my last chance tonight,' the gambler said, then threw all the dollars in his pile into the pot. Nick judged his stake to be at least $200.

The sweaty man said nothing as he fingered his cards. Then he placed them down, picked them up, mopped his brow with a kerchief that was even wetter than his brow, considered his cards some more, shrugged as if he was about to give in, then eventually nodded.

'I'm in,' he said in a small voice that broke before he coughed and cast an apologetic glance around. 'If you don't mind, that is.'

As he slowly counted out his stake, even rummaging in his pockets to make up the last few dollars in small change, Jackson considered him with bemusement. His brow furrowed as he probably pondered, like everyone else watching, whether this man was the least competent player he'd ever met, or the best. Then he shrugged and reached into his pocket. He withdrew a wad of dollars that was bigger than Nick had ever seen in Jackson's hand, then hurled them into the pot.

'So am I,' he reported confidently.

And so, with some theatrics for the benefit of the watching audience they'd laid down their cards. The gambler had a full house, kings over threes. The sweaty man bemoaned his ill luck in having only two pair. Jackson had four tens.

Jackson reached for the pot, but with timing that would have been dramatic if he hadn't mumbled his words then dropped his cards twice before turning them over, the sweaty man reported that both of his pairs were queens.

The gambler laughed with a single snort, shaking his head. The deputy didn't react at all, but Nick was only interested in Jackson's reaction.

Several hundred dollars were on the table, an order of magnitude above the stakes for which Jackson usually played. But Jackson merely looked at the four queens, then poked them apart and commended the sweaty man on his play. He stood, nodded to each of the players, and headed to the bar.

Nick watched his dignified exit as did the other players and Nick expected his mask to slip away when he reached the bar and ordered a drink. But Jackson merely downed his whiskey, considered his empty glass with a rueful smile, then slammed it down on the bar and headed outside.

On a normal evening Nick's natural inquisitiveness would have encouraged him to stay in the saloon to see if the gambler and his potential accomplice met up later to share the proceeds of their successful operation, but not tonight.

He waited a cautious minute, then headed outside. Jackson, like all the railroad employees, would be sleeping in the station house tonight and by now he should be half-way to the station, but Nick couldn't see him.

He hurried out into the road and ran his gaze down the boardwalks but still he didn't see Jackson. He couldn't have gone far in a minute, but only when Nick turned on his heel did he see him, and he was walking down the centre of the road, heading in the opposite direction to the station.

If Nick hadn't already been intrigued he would now have become excited. He slipped back onto the boardwalk, then paced down it at an unconcerned pace. Shortly afterwards Jackson left town.

Nick followed to the edge of the boardwalk and stopped, watching his form fade in the moonlight until the gloom shrouded his figure. With no protective cover to hide him, he had no choice but to follow and risk that Jackson wouldn't turn round. He hurried after him, keeping 200 yards or so back and soon discovered Jackson's destination.

A river snaked by out of town and before the cusp of one curve there was a small shack, its roof glistening in the low moonlight. Jackson was heading for this shack and Nick watched his progress until he entered it.

Fifty yards from the shack there were the collapsed remnants of a fence. Nick stopped and knelt behind the rotting wood while he considered his next move. Jackson could just be planning to sleep there, staying apart from the other railroad staff, but he had just bet more money than he should ever have owned. And he had not appeared in the least bit concerned when he had lost that money.

But having considered this, Nick was unsure as to how he could use that information. After some consideration he decided the simplest plan was to sneak up to the building and find a place where he could look in and see what Jackson was doing.

Nick stood and locked his gaze on its blank walls while trying to devise the excuse he would use if Jackson were to emerge and ask him what he was doing. But then he heard a rustling behind him. He started to turn but in a rush two heavy footfalls pounded and hard steel jabbed into the small of his back.

'Make one move,' a voice grunted in his ear, 'and it'll be your last.'

*　*　*

'Where is he?' Annie asked anxiously, ignoring the pessimistic view that Cassidy had expressed about his brother. 'What will he be — ?'

Bret cut her off with an admonishing hand then pointed to the door.

'I will find out the answers to those

questions,' he commanded. 'You will go to your room.'

'I'm a grown woman,' she said, her foot-stamp and petulant jutting of her bottom lip belying her comment. 'You can't make me do that no more.'

'I know you're all grown-up or we wouldn't have this problem, but Cassidy won't speak again until after you've left.'

Bret shot Cassidy a glance that requested his assistance and in response Cassidy folded his arms and clamped his mouth shut. Annie looked at each man in turn, but on receiving nothing but firm glares she turned on her heel, then flounced out the room with as much dignity as she could muster. Presently a door slammed some distance away. Bret sighed, then turned to Cassidy and asked the same questions as Annie had tried to ask.

'I haven't seen Emerson for ten years,' Cassidy said. 'Never had a hankering to see him again.'

Bret considered this information, then gestured outside.

'But you heard him say that to some other woman — that she should wait for him to return when the moon was new?'

'I sure did.' Cassidy glanced at Chalk as he passed him and provided him with a rueful smile. 'And I may have taunted you before, but know this — I do know how you feel.'

Chalk sneered as he joined Cassidy and Bret in heading outside. Lomax didn't move at first, but then barged ahead of them as, with another display of his surly demeanour, he showed he had no interest in this matter.

'You've got no idea,' Chalk grumbled, watching Lomax walk on ahead to his horse.

'But I have. Emerson said it to Lorna — my woman — after he stole her away from me and before he left her. My elder brother always had to have what I had and that included my woman. Afterwards, we couldn't wed. I, because I couldn't forgive her. And Lorna, because . . . well, she was always looking out for him to return.'

Chalk stomped to a halt in the doorway. 'And he didn't?'

'Of course not. I heard she'd wed someone else a year or so later, but I reckon, ten years on, she still probably looks out once a month and hopes to see him riding in with the moon at his back.'

'And he won't get that chance with Annie because I'm going to find him and tear him to pieces.'

Cassidy offered a supportive grunt. 'I know the feeling. I spent months looking for him, but I eventually admitted I was more angry with myself and with her than with him. I guess you'll feel like that one day too.'

Chalk muttered and complained some more. Bret let him speak his mind, but by the time Lomax had mounted his horse and was riding out through the ranch gates, without exchanging another word with them, Chalk started to repeat himself. Bret quietened him with a raised hand and spoke up.

'Do you want to stand here telling us

all the things you'll do to Emerson when you find him, or do you want to get that search under way?' Bret pointed to the low moon, still shining brightly in the twilit sky. 'We ain't got much more light tonight.'

'We get him,' Chalk said, with a firm slap of his fist into a palm.

Bret nodded then turned to Cassidy.

'Are you prepared to tell us any information about your brother that'll help our search?' he asked.

'If I weren't on Luther Manson's trail, I'd join you.' Cassidy considered, then shrugged. 'But I guess you could just ask around until you find another irate rancher and wronged suitor. If he hasn't changed in ten years, it won't be long before his roving eye seeks out another woman.'

'Obliged.'

'Just make sure,' Cassidy said, offering a smile to Chalk before he paced off the porch, 'you give him an extra punch from me.'

Chalk snorted and turned away.

Cassidy watched him, seeing him pout and roll his shoulders before he headed to a line of horses by the barn.

'We'll do more than punch him,' Bret said. 'There's still the matter of the murder of my friend James Glover. It's a mighty odd coincidence that Emerson left town on the same day that he was killed. If that ain't a coincidence, Emerson might not want us to find him and bring him back.'

Cassidy shook his head. 'Coincidences are always odd, but Emerson's no killer, and you can't claim he is just because he left town in a hurry.'

Bret opened his mouth as if he was about to deny this and then detail his suspicions, but as Chalk returned at that moment with three horses in tow, he thought better of it and shrugged.

'Either way, Emerson has plenty of questions to answer.'

'Provided,' Chalk grunted, holding out the reins of one of the horses to Cassidy, 'he can still speak after I've dealt with him.'

Cassidy considered each man in turn. He was pleased that they were lending him a horse so he could return to town, but what he saw in each man's cold eyes didn't fill him with hope for Emerson's chances.

These men were used to running their lives their way and handing out their version of justice. Cassidy had seen how the logic of such justice worked and a man who had wronged them was already in their eyes guilty of crimes far beyond his actual misdemeanour. Cassidy made an instant decision.

'I'm coming with you,' he said.

'I thought you were going after Luther Manson,' Bret said.

'I am, but so is Sheriff McGill and I reckon he probably doesn't want me in the way while he's trying to find him and James Glover's widow. I reckon I should leave him to it while I help you find Emerson.'

Chalk grunted his irritation, but Bret flashed him a narrow-eyed glance that preceeded a smile and a knowing nod. Cassidy pretended not to notice; he had caught the inference that they'd take his help, but when they'd found Emerson they'd deal with him in their own particular way.

'Which way then, Cassidy?' Bret asked, holding his hand out as he invited Cassidy to choose the route out of the Devil's Ridge ranch.

Ideally, Cassidy would have chosen to start searching at first light tomorrow, but as these impetuous men clearly didn't want to wait, they would still have the moon lighting their way for several hours. Cassidy stood by his new horse, a calm bay, pondering as he looked around. He could just pick out Lomax's distant form in the gloom. He looked at the darkened plains surrounding the ranch, then up to the outline of the Devil's Ridge.

In truth, the Emerson he had known had still been a youngster when he'd left home and even then he hadn't understood him. Whether he'd matured or changed in the last ten years was a secondary matter to the simple fact that his brother's motivations had been and still were a mystery to him.

But Cassidy had tracked down plenty of men before as a lawman and this situation was no different. With that in mind, his roving gaze returned to the ranch house and picked out Annie, who was loitering in the shadows beyond the doorway, watching them prepare to leave.

'I'll tell you in a moment.' Cassidy set off back to the house.

Annie flinched then backtracked into the house, but Cassidy could see her shadow on the floor.

'Hey,' Chalk grumbled from behind him, 'why the delay?'

Cassidy blocked Chalk's complaint from his mind and paced into the doorway to face her. He smiled.

'Don't you go worrying yourself while we're away,' he said.

She looked up, a mixture of hope and pleading in her watery gaze.

'Please see that he comes to no harm,' she said.

'Can't promise that. Chalk is mighty aggrieved.' He watched her gulp and lower her head. 'But I will find him and keep him alive. That I can promise.'

She looked up and gave a slight smile. 'I trust you, but only because you're his brother, so that means you must be a decent man too.'

Cassidy glanced over his shoulder to avoid her seeing his irritation in hearing her compare him favourably to his brother. He saw that Bret and Chalk had mounted up. They were out of hearing range, although both men were glaring at him. He turned back.

'You know what I want to ask you. Now that I've promised to bring him back safely, can you tell me what I want to know?'

She shook her head. 'I don't know where he is, if that's what you mean.'

'Any idea, clue, thought?' Cassidy shrugged as she continued to shake her head, then lowered his head to share her eye-line and offered her his friendliest smile. 'If I'm going to bring him back any time soon, I need somewhere to start.'

The mention of time made her flinch and she brushed back an errant strand of hair with a shaking hand.

'You have to hurry. You must get him back here quickly. He has to be here for me to . . . You must.'

Cassidy considered her tightly pressed lips, accepting that she wouldn't provide an answer as to why there was an urgency.

'I'll do my best, but he's been gone for a week. He could be many miles away by now.'

She gulped and looked around him towards Bret and Chalk, then lowered her head, her mouth moving as she conducted a silent debate with herself.

'You won't tell my father about what I've said, will you?'

'You ain't said nothing yet,' Cassidy snorted, then nodded and lowered his voice. 'But no, whatever you tell me is between the two of us.'

She didn't reply immediately and in the sultry heat of the early evening Cassidy could feel the gazes of his fellow manhunters boring into his back, but he didn't press her. He reckoned anything he said could make her quieten permanently.

'He hasn't been gone for a week,' she whispered at last. 'He came back two nights ago.'

'Your father will have to know that,' he said, but when she bored her imploring gaze into him, he continued, 'but not just yet.'

'Why must he know that, ever?'

'Because Bret reckons he killed James Glover, and in my experience a man who doesn't run is often innocent.'

'But he is innocent. We were . . . we were together when James was murdered — until Father returned.' She looked past Cassidy to the two mounted men and her voice broke several times as she recalled that night.

'Father came back from town earlier than I expected, shouting out that someone had killed James Glover. Emerson tried to leave without him seeing him, but Chalk had returned too and . . . I suppose you can guess the rest.'

She shuffled a pace back into the house, the darkness all but swallowing her form, but from the way she shook her head, she was sighing, Cassidy could deduce the way that night had gone. After Emerson had escaped Annie had tried to explain herself but the obstinate Bret and Chalk had got a completely different version of events into their heads. He leaned forward and gave her arm a reassuring pat.

'Don't you worry,' he said. 'I'll find him. We'll be gone for three nights. Then we'll return if we haven't found him and rethink our plans, but we will leave again and we will keep on looking. And I will bring him back to you, alive.'

With that promise, Cassidy turned on his heel, headed back to his horse, and mounted up.

'She tell you anything?' Chalk said, glaring at the door although Annie had now wandered back into the shadowy depths of the ranch house.

'Nope.'

'Then you've got no idea where to go.'

'I didn't say that.' Cassidy hurried his horse on. 'I know exactly where he'll be.'

Bret and Chalk followed him. In a straggling line they rode through the ranch gates and down on to the trail to Beaver Ridge, keeping the Devil's Ridge to their side. Chalk questioned Cassidy repeatedly as to where he was leading them, but Cassidy wanted to put his thoughts in order and he ignored him. At last Chalk quietened, letting Cassidy think through what he'd learnt.

Despite Annie's minimal help, she had revealed plenty, and maybe even where Emerson would be. She had spoken of the urgency of Emerson's returning and although she hadn't given a reason, Cassidy provided his own explanation. She feared she was with child and, being too scared to tell her father, Emerson was the only person she would talk to.

The fact that Emerson might have sired a child didn't sound to Cassidy like a new occurrence, but it suggested that Emerson must have been around town for several weeks, which was longer than he'd have expected him to stay.

He had also returned several days after a major altercation and that also sounded like atypical behaviour for his brother. All this suggested that he might have real feelings for Annie. Perhaps for the first time in his life he might be planning to do what he'd promised he'd do and so had stayed close to the ranch, perhaps even holing up at Devil's Ridge. Right now he might really be waiting for the right moment to ride down to her with the moon at his back.

'So,' Cassidy said when they'd ridden for an hour, 'what's the quickest route from here to Devil's Ridge?'

Bret looked back over his shoulder. 'We've been heading away from the ridge for the last half-hour.'

'Then it's about time we turned round and headed there.'

Bret nodded and turned his horse, but Chalk grunted with annoyance.

'I was right,' he said, 'Cassidy wouldn't help us find his brother. We've nearly used up the last of the light while he led us off in the wrong direction.'

Cassidy didn't give that complaint the dignity of an answer, but Bret spoke up.

'We're on a manhunt,' he said, 'and you've got to use your mind first and your anger last. Cassidy has just led us on a route that'll put anyone watching us off the trail of where we're really going.' He glanced at Cassidy. 'That is what you're doing, isn't it?'

'Yup,' Cassidy said.

'And so now I have to be the one who asks, where is our final destination?'

Cassidy pointed towards the faint outline of the ridge ahead then kept his finger moving slowly to trace out a shape.

'We left the ranch and rode on for an hour. Now we're turning and heading to the ridge. Then we head around the ridge and . . . ' Cassidy drew his horse to a halt and considered Bret as he completed his tracing of a square.

Bret nodded and favoured Cassidy with a wide smile, his teeth shining in the gloom, but Chalk's eyes flared before he brought his rising anger under control with a firm slap of his thigh.

'You saying,' he shouted, 'we just head on back to the ranch without even searching for him?'

'Sure am.'

'What's he mean, Bret?' Chalk blustered. 'What's he mean?'

'I believe,' Bret said, 'that he's suggesting Emerson really will return to the ranch, and that he'll do it tonight.'

'That's my idea,' Cassidy said.

'And you got that from Annie?' Chalk demanded.

Cassidy kept his jaw firm as he shook his head.

'Nope. Nothing she said gave me any hint that he will come back, but I just reckon he's been waiting out on the ridge for the last week, waiting for a chance to move in. I told her we'd be away for three nights and — '

'You're saying,' Chalk shouted, 'Annie will get a message to him and tell him we're gone so he can join her. You can't say that about her. She wouldn't — '

'Be quiet, Chalk,' Bret said. 'Cassidy is just using his head to think this through and I agree with him. We take a careful route back to the ranch then wait for him to show.'

Chalk muttered several complaints, but eventually he gave a grunt and a firm slap of his holster.

'And then,' he said, 'we'll sure make him regret coming back.'

'And on that,' Bret said, hurrying his

horse on, 'we can all agree.'

Cassidy watched the two men leave, leaning forward in the saddle and shaking his head, then he followed them.

5

'Don't shoot,' Nick bleated.

'Then talk,' a voice grunted in his ear, the man grinding in the gun barrel for additional emphasis.

'About what? I . . . I . . . I've got no idea what you want.'

The man slapped a hand on his shoulder and swung him round to face him, but kept the gun aimed at his chest. Nick just had enough time to recognize his assailant as being the flint-eyed deputy from the poker-game when the man spoke up.

'I'm Deputy Lomax, and I want to know what you're doing.'

'I'm just going that-a-way.' Nick pointed with a shaking hand towards the shack.

'Don't care about that. You see, I've heard you've been acting mighty suspicious, eyeing people up and following them. I reckon you've got yourself a guilty conscience and the sooner you unburden yourself about why you sold out to Luther Manson, the sooner we can get all friendly like.'

'I didn't do that,' Nick spluttered, stumbling away from Lomax in shock, but the deputy dragged him back. 'I had the same idea as you. Someone on the train *did* sell out to Luther Manson, and I was following him.'

'And why would a kid like you do that?'

'I'm a correspondent for the Eagle Heights *Chronicle*,' Nick said, surprising himself with how confident he sounded, especially as his declaration was untrue. 'And I was following up a lead on a story.'

For long moments Lomax stared down at Nick, his sneering upper lip conveying his doubt.

'You'll have to do better than that, kid.'

'Then all I can say is this: I've worked out who did it.' Nick pointed back over his shoulder. 'It was Jackson Dyer, the man who lost in that poker-game, and he headed in there.'

Lomax darted his gaze up to follow Nick's directions to the shack down by the river. He shook his head.

'That man was a fool. He got taken by the worst cardsharks I've ever had the misfortune to meet. He wouldn't be the kind to sell out to Luther.'

'Except he didn't bat an eyelid when he lost more money than he's ever had.'

A smidgen of doubt crossed Lomax's features as he nodded slowly.

'Those gamblers were from the train and I only joined that game to check them out. Then I saw you watching them ... But perhaps I might have been watching the wrong people.' Lomax patted Nick's shoulder then moved to walk past him. 'Stay here while I check Jackson out.'

'I can't do that.' Nick drew himself up to his full height and looked Lomax in the eye. 'I'm a correspondent and it was my investigative work that found him. I want to be there when you arrest him.'

Lomax considered Nick through narrowed eyes, then blew out a long sigh of exasperation. When he spoke again Nick reckoned he caught a hint of respect in his tone.

'You can get your story, kid, but remember this: a kid like you who doesn't pack a gun ain't in a position to defend himself, and I won't waste my time doing it for you. So just stay out of my way.'

With Nick walking a few paces behind the deputy, they headed down to the shack. Lomax took a meandering route, staying hunched and moving slowly and silently through the night. Nick matched his actions until Lomax stopped beside the door. Here, he held up a hand, ordering Nick to halt, then peered in through a crack between two boards. Faint light emerged from within illuminating his face with a single line of brightness.

Lomax rocked his head from side to

side, looking around the room. He edged away from the wall and gestured to Nick with two fingers held high then widened his eyes in a silent order for him to stay where he was.

Nick was still wondering what the two fingers meant when Lomax drew his gun, jumped to the side, kicked open the door, and hurtled inside.

'Reach!' he roared, brandishing his gun.

From within, Jackson bleated that he wasn't doing anything and at the same time another man spoke up, also protesting his innocence.

Nick realized that Lomax's signal had informed him that Jackson had company as Lomax issued orders for the two men inside to kneel on the floor. Nick knew he ought to stay where he was, but he figured he'd never become a correspondent if he didn't see everything that took place first hand. So when several seconds had passed and he was sure the men inside wouldn't put up a fight, he slipped into the doorway.

Inside, Jackson was kneeling with his head drooping down so that his chin rested on his chest, but the other man was kneeling with his head held high. He was facing Lomax, having assumed what Nick took to be a relaxed posture — as if he'd chosen to kneel because he wanted to — and he even had the suggestion of a smile on his face.

As Nick entered the room, Jackson rocked his head up and his eyes met Nick's, that gaze being more worried than accusing. Nick felt a twinge of guilt so he couldn't return that gaze for long and instead shuffled to the side to stand beside Lomax.

'You're Jackson Dyer,' Lomax said, receiving a confirmatory nod, then gestured with his gun to the other man. 'But I don't recognize you.'

The man looked at Lomax without any sign of concern showing in his eyes then offered a smile before he spoke.

'I'm Cassidy Yates,' he said.

'So,' Lomax said, with a snort, 'you're Cassidy Yates? And would that be Sheriff Cassidy Yates from Monotony?'

'Yup.'

'Sheriff Cassidy Yates, the brother of Emerson Yates?' Lomax considered the man until he gave a rueful smile.

'Have you ever met this Emerson Yates?'

'Nope.' Lomax licked his lips, relishing his next comment. 'But I've met Cassidy, and he's told me all about his no-good lying brother Emerson.'

The man chuckled. 'Don't believe everything you hear.'

'I don't, but as I already know that you're a liar, Emerson Yates, you're going to have to back up everything you tell me from now on to convince me you're telling the truth.'

'About any subject in particular?'

Lomax didn't reply immediately, pacing up and down instead. Nick hadn't fully understood that exchange. Although as he knew that Sheriff Cassidy Yates had recently been arrested, the fact that this man was his brother suggested his theories about Jackson Dyer were well founded.

But if Emerson was in league with Jackson and so also in league with Luther Manson, he still showed no sign of concern in his eyes and he still kept his posture casual.

'I want to know where Luther Manson is,' Lomax said at last. 'I want to know what happened to Katherine Glover. And I want to know who killed James Glover.'

'Good questions. I suggest you investigate and find out the answers.'

Lomax glanced at Jackson, who was now gulping and fidgeting, then turned his gaze back on to the calm Emerson.

'I have. That's why I'm talking to you.'

'Then I don't know how I can prove to *you* that I know nothing.'

Nick caught Emerson's emphasis, but before he could ponder on its meaning, Jackson spoke up for the first time and grunted his approval.

'He's right,' he said. 'The likes of you ain't got no right to question us.'

'I've got no idea what that's supposed

to mean. I'm Sheriff McGill's deputy and you will answer my questions. And you will start with explaining where you got your stake for that poker-game.'

'You really want me to answer that?' Jackson chuckled. 'Bearing in mind that we're both in Tex Beatty's pay.'

Lomax's face reddened and he advanced a determined pace towards Jackson with his gun raised.

'Whatever you say,' he grunted, 'my first responsibility is to the law, whereas you . . . '

'Are just the same as you.'

Lomax stopped and sneered, but Nick chose that moment to take a pace forward also and, as if his footfall had suddenly reminded Lomax of his presence, he snapped round to face him. He stared at him, his brow furrowed as if he was thinking deeply before he spoke.

'Nick,' he said, 'I need your help. Head into town, find Deputy Kendrick, and tell him to come here.'

Nick looked at the two prisoners,

both disarmed and kneeling on the floor with their shoulders hunched. He shuffled closer to Lomax and lowered his voice.

'They haven't got much fight in them. We can get them back to town. I might not have been in a situation like this before, but I can at least watch them. Trust me. They can walk in front of us and — '

'Stop telling me how to do my job.' Lomax glared at him, but then softened his voice. 'I wouldn't be a lawman if I risked your life, would I?'

'I guess not. But I reckon you can — '

'Kid, you've got a whole heap of talk in you, but be quiet for once and get Kendrick out here so that he can . . . ' Lomax licked his lips and grinned. 'So that he can help me question these men and get to the truth.'

'All right,' Nick said. 'I'll bring him back as soon as — '

'You don't need to come back. Just get that message to him then . . . then just do whatever you want to do.'

Nick could see the warning in Lomax's eyes that he'd annoyed him more than he should have, but he couldn't help but ask one last question.

'Like sell my story to the *Chronicle?*'

Lomax's eyes flared with momentary shock, before he shrugged.

'Yeah, why not? Tell Henry Sinclair the whole story, but just get out of my sight real quick and get that message to Kendrick.'

Nick nodded, then hurried to the door. He moved to go outside, but then stopped to look back. Jackson looked up at him with his eyes watery and pleading, although what he was asking him to do Nick didn't know. Lomax was smirking and for the first time Emerson was considering the deputy without the smile that had so far played on his lips.

Nick shook away the sudden burst of dread that rose up into his mind and hurried out into the night.

He sprinted back to town as fast as he could while trying to clarify in his own mind what he'd just seen and heard. Jackson Dyer and Emerson Yates were working together, he decided. They were probably in league with Luther Manson in helping him to kidnap Katherine Glover. Worse, as both Jackson and Lomax were in the pay of Tex Beatty, Tex might be implicated in that abduction too and so perhaps even in James Glover's murder.

Nick reached town before he had put those thoughts into an order that presented a firm conclusion, but he temporarily abandoned his pondering to concentrate on his first decision. He slid to a halt outside the sheriff's office, torn between going in to see Deputy Kendrick and his burning desire to go to the newspaper office.

Duty won through, but he was delighted when Kendrick was in and needed only the minimum of details before he barged past him and hurried out of town, leaving Nick to hurry on to the *Chronicle* office. And in the minute it took him to reach the office, his break from worrying at the details let him fit the information he'd acquired into a coherent story to sell.

He threw back the office door to find Henry was still sitting where he'd left him several hours ago, halfdozing with the nearly empty whiskey bottle at his side. Henry started, looked up, and frowned.

'I thought you'd be back,' he said, pausing to deliver a long yawn then drag his watch out of his waistcoat pocket. 'Didn't think you'd be back this quickly though. What you got to sell me this time?'

'I've got a real story to sell,' Nick said, 'and this time I'm the first with it. Tex Beatty is behind James Glover's murder and Katherine Glover's kidnapping — and that has to be a story you'll want to buy.'

*　*　*

Five yards to Cassidy's side, Chalk was glaring at the red orb of the sun, which was now poking out from further down the Devil's Ridge. Then he turned to Cassidy, the light harshening his sneering features.

'Now that sure was a waste of time,' he muttered. 'Emerson ain't going to show now.'

Cassidy didn't bother replying that patience was a necessity when staking out a quarry and instead continued to stare down at the ranch. One night was nothing when compared to the three weeks he'd waited for Weaver Dale to show, but just because Cassidy was patient, it didn't mean he didn't share Chalk's frustration.

They had taken turns keeping watch all night, but without any luck. Cassidy didn't think that Annie had lied to him about having met Emerson two days ago. So to have kept their liaisons private for so long, she must have used signals that let her tell him when it was safe to come to the ranch.

Sure enough, in the dead of night, a light had appeared briefly at Annie's window, disappeared, then returned twice more. It could just have been her moving around and happening to pass by the window three times with a lamp in hand, but Cassidy had judged that as being the signal.

But Emerson had not taken up her invite, if that's what it had been. They had been stealthy enough to mean he was unlikely to have seen them, and now that daylight had returned, Cassidy reckoned Emerson had decided not to risk returning on the first night after they'd left. He judged that tonight would be the most likely night of the supposed three nights available to him for him to return.

A single glance at Chalk's glaring features convinced him this opinion would fall on deaf ears.

'Patience, patience,' Bret said from further down the ridge. 'This may take days, not hours.'

'I ain't got that much patience.' Chalk slipped back from the edge and stood. 'I'm going after him.'

'And how will you do that?' Cassidy asked. 'You have no trail, no leads, no clues.'

Chalk opened and closed his mouth as he searched for an answer.

'I sure don't know that but I do know he won't come back in daylight and I ain't chilling my butt up here all day.'

Bret shook his head, sighing, but Cassidy spoke up first.

'Perhaps dividing during daylight is a good idea,' he said.

Bret swirled his head round to look at him, his eyebrows raised in surprise, but a grunted oath from Chalk confirmed that Cassidy's attempt to mollify him wouldn't work.

'I ain't dividing,' he muttered, pacing down the ridge to stand over Cassidy and so placing himself squarely against the skyline for anyone to see who happened to be down below them. 'I've had enough of your plans. I'll get him on my own. What you think of that?'

'I think any damn fool who ain't got the sense to keep his head down when staking out a man could search for ever and never find nobody.'

Chalk's face reddened, but despite Cassidy's admonishment he didn't step away from the edge. He continued to glare down at Cassidy, then spat out several wellchosen oaths before storming off to his horse.

Cassidy looked at Bret, hoping to share a moment of mutual agreement about the impetuous Chalk, but Bret rolled to his knees then crawled away from the edge too. He stopped beside Cassidy.

'I guess,' he said, 'I'll be going too.'

'Bret, you know waiting here is the best way of finding him, and you know traipsing around with that idiot is the best way of ensuring you'll never find Emerson.'

Bret's eyes flared and Cassidy instantly saw that he'd overstepped himself and so lost any chance of finding common ground with him.

'That's Annie's betrothed you're talking about and he's a better man than your no-good brother will ever be.'

Cassidy reckoned there wasn't much to choose between them, but he kept that thought to himself.

'Whatever you and I may think of Emerson, I reckon he and Annie care for each other.' Cassidy glanced at Chalk, who had now reached his horse. 'And last night Chalk and Annie didn't appear to me as if they were two people who enjoy each other's company. Makes me wonder why he is so determined to believe that she is his woman.'

Cassidy had hoped his comment might placate Bret, but it had the opposite effect. Bret snorted his breath, his eyes flaring. He darted in closer to Cassidy, his jaw rippling as he fought to control his anger. Then in a moment that was gone almost before Cassidy could register what he'd seen, Bret's eyes flickered with an emotion — and Cassidy reckoned he understood it. It was doubt. And in that moment Cassidy understood the cause of Bret's anger, and perhaps even his greatest fear.

Chalk didn't care for Annie, after all, but he did care for the land and the wealth that would come with her hand. Worse, Bret knew this, but wouldn't admit it to himself, and now he had transferred his anger at the situation into a hatred of someone who was clearly less suitable for his daughter than even Chalk was.

'I sure know,' Bret snapped, 'that Chalk cares for her more than Emerson did before he hightailed it out of here. But that don't matter now. I was prepared to accept your hunch last night, but now I'll take my own hunch that as Emerson killed James Glover, he won't stay around here waiting for us to dry-gulch him.'

As Bret crawled away, Cassidy asked a quick question that didn't halt him.

'What evidence have you got that Emerson killed him?'

'Emerson threatened James,' Bret called over his back.

Cassidy wanted to quiz Bret some more, but as Bret stood up, then joined Chalk by his horse, he had to accept that Bret had said all he would on the subject.

Cassidy watched them leave on what he reckoned was a futile chase. Bret didn't so much as look at him again as he rode off, although Chalk paused to look back and smirk, as if he'd won an important victory now that Bret had chosen to go with him.

But despite his delight Cassidy also saw the look in Chalk's eyes that he'd seen in Bret's, and now that he thought about it, he had seen Bret and Chalk trade doubt several times, and perhaps even shame. Or perhaps it was just an unwillingness to look a man straight in the eye that men who had something to hide always had.

By the time both men had disappeared from view, Cassidy was sure he knew what Chalk was hiding — his lack of interest in Annie and his interest in the Devil's Ridge ranch. And so, for perhaps the first time in his life, he felt a tremor of affinity with his brother. He might not like him, or trust him, or for that matter even want to see him again, but at least he wasn't as odious as Chalk was.

He even entertained the thought that maybe after he'd found Emerson and proved he wasn't a killer, it might be worth his time to try to help him and Annie reconcile.

For the next few hours Cassidy watched the Devil's Ridge ranch. Although he stayed, he did agree with Bret and Chalk that Emerson probably wouldn't return during the daylight hours, but he didn't reckon scouting around would achieve anything other than to alert him if he happened to be nearby.

But with nothing else to occupy his mind, as the morning wore on Bret's conviction that Emerson was involved in James Glover's death started to dwell on his mind. Unless Annie was lying about the events of last week, Emerson was clearly innocent of that crime, but proving it would only help Emerson if he, Cassidy, were the first man to find him.

The sun had yet to reach its highest point when Cassidy also slipped back from the edge of the ridge and mounted his horse. Then he headed off taking a protected and circuitous route down the back of Devil's Ridge, his ultimate destination Eagle Heights.

6

In a matter of minutes the current week's issue of the Eagle Heights *Chronicle* would be available, and Nick could hardly contain his excitement.

It had been late into the night when Henry had shooed him out of the office, stating he didn't need his help with the typesetting and printing of the final version with his efficient new linotype machine.

Nick had then loitered outside the sheriff's office for another hour, hoping to see Deputy Lomax return with his prisoners, but his tiredness defeated him and he retired to the station where he slept fitfully. He had awoken early and paced up and down outside Arthur McIntyre's mercantile, planning to be the first to read a copy. Even so, he wasn't the first in the queue and he struck up conversations with the men around him, hoping he would get the chance to mention casually that the lead article this week would be his story.

Nobody presented him with that opportunity, but he dismissed that irritation from his mind when he had the *Chronicle* in his hand and he could at last steal himself to read his first ever story in print.

But he held back from enjoying that pleasure and calmly tucked the paper under his arm. He paced down the boardwalk to the end. Then, acting as casually as he could, as if he was just anyone reading the paper, he leaned on the corner post and flicked the paper open. He read the headline.

It was about James Glover's murder, but didn't mention what Nick had uncovered last night. Nick scanned down the page searching for the point where Henry had mingled his tale in, but he hadn't. There was no mention of Jackson Dyer and Deputy Lomax being in Tex Beatty's pay, or of Jackson having helped Luther Manson to kidnap Katherine Glover, or of the possible links between Emerson Yates and James Glover's murder. And there was certainly no mention of Nick's conclusion that Tex Beatty had been behind everything that had happened here recently.

Then he read the other items on the front page, but none of them was his story either. He had expected news of the magnitude he'd uncovered to be on the front page, but with the first tremor of a worrying dread fluttering in his guts, he decided that late news probably went on the second page.

The story wasn't on the second page either, or the third. In fact it wasn't on any page.

Nick thrust the pages back and forth with ever more frantic gestures as he searched for his story. He read every single article, no matter how irrelevant, as he looked for even a scrap of information referring to what he'd seen and heard last night.

It took Nick a full half-hour of reading before he finally accepted the truth. He might have sold his first story to the Eagle Heights *Chronicle*, but Henry hadn't printed it.

★   ★   ★

Cassidy's first destination when he arrived in Eagle Heights was the sheriff's office, where he hoped to find Sheriff McGill and confirm that he now accepted that the charges against him were untenable.

McGill was out of town on the trail of Luther Manson, although Deputy Kendrick was in and he grumpily advised him that he had informed the sheriff about what had happened last night. Cassidy guessed that he hadn't told him all the details and he resolved to inform McGill of Lomax's behaviour when he got the chance. But the bruised cheek, black eye and scraped knuckles Kendrick was nursing suggested this deputy might not be in the mood to hear Cassidy's complaints.

Having been on the receiving end of Lomax's brutal methods, neither did Cassidy enquire about how Lomax's fellow deputy had acquired his bruises. But he did allow himself a sigh of relief after hearing the news that he was no longer a wanted man.

Once outside, he was minded to head to the saloon to search for people to question about James Glover's murder, but the newspaper pile outside Arthur's mercantile caught his attention first. So he leaned back against the wall outside the store and read the reported details.

They were simple and familiar.

James had been drinking in the saloon, as was his wont when his wife was out of town. He had left the saloon early, claiming a prior engagement, but everyone in the saloon had heard a single shot moments later.

Numerous people had hurried out on to the road to find that aside from the mortally wounded James, nobody else was outside. The deeply concerned and, according to the newspaper, distraught and inconsolable respected local businessman Tex Beatty had reached the body first, although where he had been earlier wasn't reported.

Tex had organized the townsfolk into a posse to find his business partner's killer, and later offered a $1,000 reward for any information that led to an arrest. As yet nobody had been found, although Sheriff McGill had identified one unnamed suspect, presumably Emerson.

The article included the testimony of several named people who had been in the saloon, including Bret Sanborn, but not Chalk Pendleton. So Cassidy resolved to find and question the other named people.

He tucked the paper under his arm and set off down the boardwalk. But he was distracted by the amusing sight of a red-faced young man standing in the road and tearing a copy of the Eagle Heights *Chronicle* into shreds with extravagant sweeps of his arms. Then he threw the shreds to the ground and even jumped on them before kicking them away.

'Feel better for that?' Cassidy said, giving a jovial grin as he passed.

The young man glared at him, then kicked the last piece of stamped-on paper away.

'Won't ever feel better after reading trash like that.'

This comment was cryptic and intriguing enough to stop Cassidy.

'You talking about the report on James Glover's murder?'

'Yeah.'

'What didn't you like about what was in there?'

'What was in there was just fine. It was the news Henry left out I didn't like.'

'What news?'

'The . . . the . . . Oh, it doesn't matter.' He turned to slouch away, but Cassidy paced to the side and blocked his way.

'If you've got information that ain't

in the *Chronicle*, I'd welcome hearing it.' He winked. 'Don't worry. You can talk to me. I'm Sheriff Cassidy Yates.'

The young man flinched back a pace. 'Sheriff Cassidy . . . Cassidy Yates?'

'Yeah, and don't go worrying yourself about my reputation. What you may have heard about me is just plain wrong. I'm no longer under arrest or under suspicion. Same can't be said for my no-good brother — '

'Emerson Yates.'

Cassidy raised his eyebrows. 'Now that's mighty knowledgeable of you. How did you get to hear about him?'

The young man told him and so, five minutes later, Cassidy hurried out of town, heading for a shack down by the river. Chalk Pendleton had told him that he had borrowed money from James Glover to buy a place for him and Annie to live in when they were wed. Despite the shack's dilapidated state, Cassidy reckoned this was Chalk's property.

As he'd expected, the place was deserted, but when he'd slipped through the broken door, he noticed that the thick dust on the floor was untouched in the corners, whereas numerous scuff-marks were in the centre of the shack. Several boards had snapped away from one wall, leaving the pieces lying outside, and the clean edges of the jagged pieces of wood suggested they'd broken off recently.

When Cassidy poked his head through the hole he found a handprint in the dirt beside the broken boards, and he concluded that someone had fallen through the wall and landed on his back. Putting this together with the scuff-marks, Cassidy reckoned a fight had broken out here, in which, according to Nick Kearney, Deputies Lomax and Kendrick had tussled with Emerson Yates and Jackson Dyer. The state of Kendrick's face suggested who had come off worse.

This still left open the question of the health of the other three, especially as Nick had reported that the deputies had been planning to question their prisoners here, a prospect that he had viewed with some concern. And which

Cassidy had viewed with even more concern.

And that concern grew when, in the shadows, Cassidy's gaze fell upon a patch of blood, now dry and brown, but nevertheless large enough to make him fear for his brother's safety.

Cassidy knelt by the dried spot of blood, fingering it as he looked round the shack. From this angle he saw the sun twinkling through several small holes in the wall, the size of bullet-holes. He also saw other spots of blood trailing to the door, suggesting a wounded man had made his way outside.

Cassidy had a knot in his stomach when he considered the likely fate of his brother after his own experience of Lomax's brutal methods. But curiously he felt even more concern when he considered what Nick Kearney had told him. He didn't trust his brother, but he'd never considered for a moment that he might be involved in the events here over the last week.

But whatever had happened, he forced himself to put his concerns from his mind and concentrate on what he could discover here. And one conclusion was obvious — Jackson and Emerson were still at large, Lomax was after them, and one of these people was injured.

Outside, Cassidy picked up several trails of footprints and spots of blood, leading away from the shack. These led ultimately to hoofprints, suggesting that Emerson had left a horse some distance from the shack. He also found other trails that suggested two people, presumably Lomax and Kendrick, had followed the trail.

Unfortunately it didn't take him long to find the reason why Kendrick had returned to town.

Five miles downriver a body lay slumped, half-in, half-out the water. From where he sat on his horse Cassidy could tell it wasn't his brother and when he jumped down and turned the body over, he didn't recognize the man, although, from the description Nick had provided, he believed it to be Jackson Dyer. A heavily bloodied side indicated the reason for his death.

Cassidy dragged the body clear of the water, then left it to pursue Lomax's and Emerson's trail. The occasional spots of blood he'd seen earlier no longer appeared, comforting him that his brother hadn't been hurt.

For most of the afternoon he followed a trail that darted in various directions, as if Emerson was trying to shake off Lomax's pursuit, and the sun was lowering when Cassidy confirmed that he had finally succeeded.

Emerson and Lomax's trails headed back into the river and despite searching along both sides, as he could see that Lomax had also done, Cassidy couldn't find where Emerson's trail emerged.

But he did confirm that Lomax had eventually relented and headed away from the river, a distinctive print-pattern proving that it was he. Cassidy followed his trail for long enough to confirm that the deputy had returned to Eagle Heights. Then Cassidy leaned forward in the saddle, staring towards town and feeling some satisfaction that his brother had thrown off the trail of this unworthy lawman.

Then he turned himself to the other matter of finding him himself. It didn't take Cassidy long to decide that the assumption he'd considered some hours ago was in fact correct.

Emerson had taken a route that had meandered in many different directions, but he had studiously avoided going anywhere near Devil's Ridge.

So, Cassidy decided, that meant Devil's Ridge was the only place he would go.

7

If the engineers had completed their repairs, so that the train had been able to resume its journey that day, Nick would have got on it straight away and returned to selling newspapers and other items to the passengers. But as he had to remain in town until the next day, he reckoned he couldn't avoid going to see Henry Sinclair.

Still, it took him several hours before he could bring himself to head to the *Chronicle* office. And as he'd spent that time stewing over his situation, when he opened the door he was in the mood to give Henry a piece of his mind.

He stood tall in the doorway, holding his chin high as he forced himself to keep calm and so be able to state everything he wanted to say before he became too upset or Henry threw him out. He waited until Henry looked up from his desk and he was surprised, but not cheered, when Henry hailed him with a wide smile and beckoned him in.

Nick slouched into the office, knowing that Henry would probably reckon he was acting like a petulant child, but not caring.

'What's wrong?' Henry said, still smiling.

'As if you don't know,' Nick murmured to himself before raising his voice to such a pitch that it broke. 'You didn't print my story.'

Henry considered this comment while nodding slowly, as if this was new information to him and he hadn't considered that Nick might be concerned when he didn't find his story in the *Chronicle*.

'I could regale you with excuses but as you want to become a correspondent, you should hear the truth. There was no story to print.'

'There was!' Nick screeched, suddenly finding himself close to tears, but no longer caring about keeping his dignity. 'The law has caught up with some of the men who helped to kidnap Katherine Glover, and Deputy Lomax reckoned they might have something to do with James Glover's murder too.'

'No story there,' Henry said as Nick paused for breath. 'What else did you have?'

'Jackson Dyer said some mighty interesting things about Tex Beatty having lawmen in his pay. Then there's . . . There's plenty of story there.'

Henry winced. 'There was certainly nothing in that to print.'

'Why not?' Nick demanded, slamming his hands on his hips.

Henry didn't reply immediately. He placed his pen on his desk and stood up, then tucked his hands behind his back and paced away to the window. He looked outside. His gaze fell on the hotel down the road — one of Tex Beatty's many establishments. When he spoke, he affected a lecturing tone.

'I find it sad that I have to explain something that should be obvious to a young man who wishes to be a correspondent. But here it is: the law apprehended two *suspects* — not guilty people. It's only conjecture that they had anything to do with James's murder and the kidnapping of Katherine Glover.' Henry took deep breaths, then turned away from the window to face Nick and for the first time, Nick saw genuine anger in his narrowed eyes. 'And the allegation that Tex Beatty is corrupt and so might be behind recent events here is so . . . so tenuous it shouldn't even be uttered.'

'But the role of the newspaper — '

'The role of my newspaper is to report the truth,' Henry roared, before lowering his voice, 'and until I hear some truth from you, I won't print a single allegation you bring to me.'

'But both Jackson Dyer and Deputy Lomax are in Tex's pay and — '

'You have no proof of that, only an overheard snippet of conversation that you might have misinterpreted. And until you have proof, I'll never print a word against Tex Beatty, or against any of these other people you want to tar with your gossip.'

'That wasn't gossip. I risked my life to get that story. I was with a lawman when he burst in on outlaws. I . . . I . . . ' Nick slapped his thigh as he tried to recall the carefully rehearsed arguments he'd put together before coming here. Then he remembered one aspect of his report that he reckoned Henry couldn't explain away. 'Then why did you buy my story?'

Henry shrugged. 'A whole heap of reasons — to encourage you, to discourage you from getting yourself into any more dangerous situations, to teach you a valuable lesson.'

'I have had enough of your valuable lessons. You don't know nothing about . . . about . . . '

As Nick struggled for words, a small voice in his mind told him to listen to what Henry had said and to admit that he was right. And he knew that when he calmed down later, he would accept that he hadn't come across a single fact last night, just hints and suggestions of a truth, and perhaps not even the actual truth. That still didn't help to overcome his anger.

'Before you say anything else you'll regret, I'll tell you this,' Henry said, his voice now soft and returning to its normal kindly tone. He considered Nick, no doubt taking in his red face, hunched shoulders, and hurt eyes. 'I accept employees speaking to me like that once, but never twice.'

'Well, that sure is fine for your employees, but as I don't . . . ' Nick closed his eyes as his mind caught up with his mouth and stopped him destroying any chance of ever reconciling himself with Henry. 'Are you saying what I think you're saying?'

'I'm saying you now work for me.'

For six months Nick had waited to hear those words, but now that he had, he was amazed to find he was still more annoyed than pleased.

'I accept,' he forced himself to say.

'But why? You ignored every word I wrote.'

'I didn't ignore your words, I just didn't print them. And I didn't print them because every word you wrote was utter trash.' Despite his harsh words, Henry winked and offered an encouraging smile. 'But you got every-thing else right. You sniffed out a potential story. You showed you've got enthusiasm. You showed you've got persistence. The only thing you didn't prove was that you're willing to learn . . .'

Henry raised his eyebrows, inviting a response.

Nick might have still been angry, but he knew when the time to back down had come.

'I sure am prepared to learn, Mr Sinclair,' he said, and was pleased to find he meant it. 'And the next time I get close to proving Tex Beatty is behind James Glover's murder, I'll bring you only the facts.'

'The next time . . .' Henry shivered,

almost as if he hoped there would never be a next time, then regained his composure by tucking his thumbs into his waistcoat and heading back to his desk. 'I'm pleased to hear it, Nick, and you can start learning what facts are by forgetting everything you think you know about newspapers.'

'I'll do that, Mr Sinclair,' Nick said, now warming to the unexpected direction this meeting had taken. He looked around the office. 'Where do you want me to start?'

Henry took a sheet of paper from his desk and held it out to him. 'First, head on down to Mrs Bradley in the saloon.'

Nick took the paper. 'Has she got a story for the *Chronicle*?'

'Nope, just read what's written there.' Henry waited until Nick started reading. 'Next week her brother will arrive in town with a hundred head of cattle to sell and I want you to clarify the details with her.'

'Cattle,' Nick murmured.

'And don't go sneering at your first

assignment,' Henry said, waggling a finger, although his lively eyes betrayed his amusement. 'Advertisements bring in the money, and money lets us print the news.'

'I'll remember that.' Nick turned to the door.

'And don't dawdle. I've got another assignment for you once you've completed that one.'

'Oh?' Nick said, turning and smiling hopefully.

'Yup.' Henry gestured to a broom propped up in the corner of the room. 'The office needs sweeping out.'

Nick couldn't help but wince, but then with a shrug and short skip he regained his enthusiasm and hurried outside. And as he hurried down the boardwalk, he whistled, pleased that at last he was on his way to his first official assignment for the Eagle Heights *Chronicle*.

★   ★   ★

The light had just gone off in Annie's window.

From high up on Devil's Ridge, Cassidy narrowed his eyes, peering intently at the ranch in the bright twilight. And as he expected, that light came then went twice more.

It was the same signal as the one she'd provided late last night, except that tonight Annie had barely waited until the sun had set before she'd given it. This suggested an urgency to which Emerson would have to respond — if he ever would. Annie believed that Bret and Chalk would return after one more night and with Deputy Lomax after him, Emerson would probably be worried enough to use this window of opportunity.

Moving silently, Cassidy made his way down the side of the ridge, keeping in the shadows that the strong moonlight cast. At ground level, below the looming Devil's Ridge, it was dark enough to move more freely and he took the route he'd planned during the daylight hours to reach the ranch's fence.

He slipped beneath the fence and took up a position between the stable wall and a horse-trough some thirty yards to the side of Annie's window. Here he would be able to see Emerson when he approached her window; no matter from which direction he came.

An hour passed without any sign of him making that attempt, but when movement came, it happened in a rush.

First, he heard a rustling to his right. Then a shape flittered through the shadows, giving Cassidy such a fleeting glimpse that he was still unsure as to whether it had been a man. He locked his gaze on the last place he'd seen that movement, noting that if it were a man, he was using the same route into the ranch as he had.

Then the movement came again, emerging from the shadows and letting Cassidy see that it was a standing man. A low murmur sounded which to Cassidy sounded like a demand to get down and accordingly the shape dropped out of sight.

Cassidy had just decided that the voice he'd heard was Bret's, which meant the other person would be Chalk, when from the opposite direction he saw movement again. He glanced to the side and saw that standing in the shadows with his back pressed against the barn wall was a man. The light-level wasn't great enough for Cassidy to see who it was, but this man had his gaze locked on Annie's window.

Stealthily, Cassidy got to his feet and headed towards him, silently placing his feet to the ground and keeping out of his line of sight. He was several paces away when the man flinched, his body darting forward as he decided to make a run for Annie's window.

But he didn't get the chance.

Cassidy took two long paces, then lunged and looped an arm around the man's chest while slapping a hand over his mouth. Then he dragged him back into the darkest shadows and finally to his knees.

He held him firmly, but the man struggled, trying to escape. So Cassidy released his hand from the man's mouth and spun him round so they could see each other. The man's fist rose, aiming to clip his chin, as Cassidy had known it would, and he had his hand in place to catch the fist and hold it as he stared into the man's eyes.

'Howdy, Emerson,' he whispered. 'It's been a while.'

8

Nick whistled a merry tune as he headed down the road towards the station to sleep amongst his former colleagues for what would be the last time. He'd been a correspondent for the Eagle Heights *Chronicle* for just a few hours, but already he felt as if he was born to do the job.

The desire still burned in him to uncover the conspiracy he suspected existed over Tex Beatty's involvement in the fate of James and Katherine Glover. But with Henry keeping him occupied, he hadn't been able to devote any time to building on what he'd learnt so far. Now he wondered whether uncovering the story, or lack of one, had fulfilled its purpose in getting him a job with the *Chronicle*. Perhaps from now on he ought to do what Henry wanted him to do and concentrate on reporting the news the right way.

Admittedly, aside from clarifying the details of a cattle sale with Mrs Bradley, the only activities Henry had allocated him were menial tasks, like sweeping out the office or making coffee, but tomorrow he would have his first real assignment.

In the morning the train would resume its journey. Henry had given him the responsibility of providing a short report on the event. So before retiring he envisaged the scene that he would face tomorrow. He worked out that standing beside the station house would be the best position to drink in the atmosphere. Henry wouldn't let him report on too much of that atmosphere, but that didn't stop him from concocting the article he'd write up tomorrow.

'Despite Luther Manson's raid and the tragic loss of a valiant passenger,' he whispered to himself, 'the brave and fearless . . . '

A shadow loomed over him and a

hand clamped down on his shoulder, then swirled him round. He found himself facing Deputies Lomax and Kendrick. Behind them, Tex Beatty loomed.

'Nick Kearney,' Lomax said, his simple statement sending a flurry of alarm rippling through Nick's stomach.

Nick hadn't seen either man since the incident last night and when he'd fought down his initial shock he couldn't help but linger his gaze on the bruises both men were displaying on their faces.

'Did you . . . ? Did you arrest those men last night?' he asked.

Lomax rubbed his chin as Tex blinked hard and bored his gaze into the back of Lomax's head.

'We didn't get the chance,' Kendrick grunted.

'Yeah,' Lomax murmured. 'The damn varmints got the drop on us and vamoosed.'

'I got word to Kendrick as fast as I could,' Nick said, darting his gaze to Kendrick, then Lomax, then the silent Tex.

Kendrick grunted a confirmation that he had done as ordered while Tex offered a brief smile.

'You don't need to go worrying yourself,' Tex said soothingly. 'I don't blame *you* for them getting away.'

Tex shot a glance at Lomax's back and although Lomax couldn't have seen it, the deputy shuffled from foot to foot.

'Yeah,' Lomax said. 'You got Kendrick's help as fast as you could, but now we want your help again.'

'Pleased to help in any way I can,' Nick said, cautiously, 'but how?'

Tex reached into his pocket and extracted a ten-dollar bill. He folded it, then slipped in between Lomax and Kendrick and tucked it into Nick's top pocket. Then he took another bill and repeated the action.

Nick reckoned he could feel the bills burning his chest, but they were so welcome he couldn't help but smile. Tex patted his shoulder.

'All the lawmen in town couldn't make progress in finding James's killer or Katherine, but you tracked down Jackson Dyer and Emerson Yates. I have a good feeling about you. I reckon you'll make a fine assistant to Henry Sinclair and I just want you to know who your friends are.'

'I do,' Nick said, fighting down the urge to ask why he was paying him for having located a man who was already in his pay.

'And as we're now friends, I want you to promise me that you'll come and see me the moment you see anything interesting.' Tex lowered his voice. 'Emerson Yates, for instance, will be worth a thousand dollars. Understand?'

Nick reckoned the presence of the three men looming around him gave him no choice but to nod. Then, with a series of pats on the back, the deputies and Tex peeled away to head off back into town.

Despite his discomfort with the encounter, a pleasant minute passed during which time Nick dreamed up numerous ways he could spend his newly acquired wealth until the idea that had dominated his thoughts last night returned to him.

Jackson Dyer had claimed Tex Beatty had paid him for an undisclosed activity, although Nick had deduced that it was for his help in Katherine Glover's kidnapping. At the time this had intrigued and disgusted Nick, but having now taken Tex's money, he had joined the ranks of Eagle Heights's townsfolk who were in his pay. He was no better than Jackson Dyer, or the surly Deputy Lomax, or . . .

A terrible thought hit him.

He fought to keep it at bay but as he watched Tex and the two deputies swing past the *Chronicle* office before heading into Tex's hotel, he couldn't explain his fear away.

Henry Sinclair was also in Tex Beatty's pay. He had refused to print the story Nick had uncovered, not because of the lack of facts, but because he couldn't print the truth about a man who controlled him. Worse, he'd bought

Nick's story then employed him and given him menial tasks to do, not because he thought he had the potential to become a correspondent, but to distract him from delving any further into Tex's activities.

Such a thought ought to have shocked Nick, but the only emotion he detected in himself was disappointment. The man whom he admired so much he almost worshipped, the only man who had ever encouraged him, and whom he wanted to emulate one day, wasn't dedicated to reporting the truth, but just to keeping out of trouble with Tex Beatty.

'No,' Nick murmured. 'I've got it wrong. Henry Sinclair stands for the truth. And I'll prove it.'

With that thought, he left the station and slowly walked back down the road. In his new belligerent state of mind he resolved to give the money away later. This helped to assuage his guilt, but if he were ever to be completely free of Tex's influence, he would have to finish the story he had started to uncover last night.

Then he would convince Henry Sinclair that he must print it and so prove that the Eagle Heights *Chronicle* stood for the truth.

But first, he needed solid facts.

Nick's gaze roved down the road until it stopped at the hotel Tex had entered. Tex owned the two hotels in town, standing next to each other. One was for the use of travellers, but Tex lived in the second, occupying the entire first floor. From what Nick had heard, Tex's friends and business acquaintances always stayed with him there, and he always provided them with plenty of entertainment.

That meant that if he were to find incriminating evidence that would prove what Tex was doing in this town, he'd find it in there.

Nick took a circuitous route past Tex's hotel. From the corner of his eye he noted that inside numerous people were downstairs, huddling around Tex, and their jovial demeanour suggested that they were embarking on one of those celebrations for which Tex was famous.

The inappropriateness of this while his business partner was unburied and while Katherine Glover's fate was still unknown added to Nick's determination that he would sneak up to the first floor and find something with which to incriminate Tex.

And while Tex was downstairs socializing would be the best opportunity he would get.

He didn't reckon he could reach the stairs unnoticed while wending his way through the people downstairs and he looked around for other avenues of entry. One soon caught his eye. He carried on past the hotel to Tex's other hotel and, as there was nobody loitering downstairs, he went inside, up the stairs and along the first-floor corridor unchallenged.

He orientated himself to the road outside then steeled himself for testing the lock on the door of the room that looked down on to that road. He was lucky in that the room was open and unoccupied and he slipped inside and to the window.

With the aid of the balcony, which nudged close to the balcony of the hotel next door, Nick slipped through the window, climbed over the gap between the balconies, and in through a window. He stood at the end of a long corridor. Doors were on either side. Stairs were at the end. He stood for a moment, listening to the merry chatter rippling away downstairs, then put himself to the task of searching through the upstairs rooms.

But then his luck ran out.

Only the room at the end of the corridor appeared to be currently occupied. Light streamed out into the darkened corridor around the edges of the door and through the keyhole. Nick also heard someone moving around inside, so he left this room unchecked, but whereas in the other hotel the unoccupied rooms had been unlocked, here all the doors were locked. Nick reckoned that this proved there were secrets to be found here, but unless he could find a way to get into the rooms, he was unlikely to uncover those secrets.

Nick half-heartedly put his shoulder to several doors, but when they all refused to open he decided that breaking in would cause too much noise and damage. Seeing no other options available, he was resigning himself to leaving unnoticed, after which he'd rethink his plans, when the occupied room again drew his attention. As he had been unable to find anything that supported his suspicions up here, he knelt before the door and put his eye to the keyhole.

For five minutes he saw only the room, which was unoccupied in the part he could see, although he could hear low breathing. Then the bed creaked and a person moved into view, coming so close to the door that the figure was just a blurred barrier that blocked his entire view. In case this person was planning to leave, he darted his head back from the door and looked around for somewhere to hide.

But footfalls receded from the door and so Nick again looked through the keyhole.

This time he saw that the person was a woman. She was dressed for bed with a shawl around her shoulders to keep out the cold. She had her back to him as she stood close to the window. She edged a draped and closed curtain aside and through the crack looked down at the road below.

She didn't move for some time until eventually she placed the curtain back down carefully and turned from the window to return to the bed.

Only then did Nick see who she was.

The woman was Katherine Glover.

★ ★ ★

'Cassidy?' Emerson murmured, his eyes bright in the gloom.

'Be quiet,' Cassidy urged. 'Bret and Chalk are over there.'

Emerson instantly stopped struggling and quietened, then held his hand to the side, inviting Cassidy to take charge.

Cassidy had only planned his route into the ranch, as he hadn't expected that he would have to make a stealthy exit, but he judged that heading in the opposite direction to Bret and Chalk was the safest option. He dropped to his knees and crawled around the side of the barn, then stood.

Emerson joined him and together they edged away from the barn. Then they darted from building to building, always staying in the shadows, until they reached the fence, some 300 yards away from the point where Cassidy had slipped under it.

By now Cassidy was itching to confront Emerson with what he'd heard about him, but he resisted the temptation. And when Emerson tried to direct him to where he'd left his horse,

Cassidy overruled him and instead led him off to the Devil's Ridge, meeting up with the route on which he'd headed to the ranch a half-mile on.

At the bottom of the ridge, he stopped to watch the ranch and confirm that they weren't being followed. Presently, as if to taunt them, a light went on in Annie's bedroom, then came and went twice more as she paraded before the window, signalling.

Emerson murmured his disquiet and this encouraged Cassidy to lead him up the side of the ridge. Ten minutes later they reached the point where Cassidy had been watching the ranch some two hours ago. There, he knelt down and looked at Emerson, letting him speak first.

'I was right, Cassidy,' Emerson said, simply. 'It has been a while.'

Cassidy snorted. 'Is that all you've got to say to me?'

'I don't know where to start.' Emerson leaned towards him, smiling. 'But if I knew where you wanted me to start, it might help.'

Cassidy had so many things he wanted to ask, but he settled for the most pressing.

'James Glover,' he said.

Emerson sighed and shuffled round to lie on his belly, looking down the ridge towards the ranch.

'I didn't kill James, if that's what's worrying you. James hired me to find out who was plotting to kill him, but he died before I could help him.'

Cassidy lay down beside him. 'And who do you reckon killed him?'

'Tex Beatty, of course.' Emerson slapped his fist on the ground. 'And don't ask me if I've got proof. I did have once but not any more. So I investigated. I worked out that Jackson Dyer was involved somehow, but before he could tell me what he knew those deputies ensured he wouldn't talk.'

'Emerson, I want to believe you, but based on what I can remember of you, I find it hard to believe you've become the kind of man whom James Glover would have hired to protect him.' Cassidy looked at Emerson until he murmured a rueful agreement. 'How did you get the job?'

'I worked for someone who knows Bret Sanborn. He had a word with Bret and he recommended me to James.'

'Now some of this is starting to sound plausible. But how did Bret get it into his head you raped his daughter and killed James?'

'The tale with Annie you can guess, but James . . . ' Emerson shuffled round to face Cassidy and when he spoke again, he used a brisk, matter-of-fact tone. 'I found this contract, proving Tex was trying to cut James out of their partnership. James was convinced this was the evidence he needed and he planned to confront Tex with it on the night Tex killed him. My agreement with James was that he'd pay me if I found any evidence, but James refused to pay up until after he'd seen Tex. I had no choice but to wait, but I wasn't . . . let's just say . . . happy about that.'

'You mean you threatened him?'

Emerson provided a rueful nod. 'I guess I said some things. I didn't mean to carry them out, but I figured James was taking advantage of me.'

'You always were impatient,' Cassidy said, unable to stop his irritation brimming over into an admonishment. 'Perhaps you're getting what you deserve. If it'd been me, I'd have waited to be paid.'

'You would,' Emerson said, conveying a considerable amount of contempt in his simple comment. 'But I wanted to leave as quickly as I could.'

'With Annie?'

'Why would I want to do that?' Emerson snapped, his eyes opening wide in astonishment.

'Then why are you still here, if you're not aiming to take Annie away with you?'

'I have to find James's killer.'

'Not to get paid, then?' Cassidy said, raising his voice as his irritation at his brother's actions grew.

'That'd sure be nice, but I can't see that happening. Even so, I reckon I at least owe it to James to prove that Tex killed him before I leave.'

Cassidy sighed. 'I don't know whether to be pleased you've got the loyalty to unmask James's killer, or to be annoyed you ain't staying for Annie. But either way, you've said nothing yet that convinces me you're telling the truth.'

'Then what else can I say?'

Cassidy licked his lips, relishing confronting Emerson with something he couldn't easily explain.

'It'd have helped if you hadn't started working for James having told him such a huge lie, wouldn't it, *Cassidy*?'

Emerson winced. 'Ah, that. It was a small lie to secure the job and then it was hard to change afterwards.' He shrugged. 'I never expected you to turn up and prove I wasn't you.'

'But why would you ever consider taking my name in the first place?' Cassidy watched Emerson open his mouth to answer. 'And don't tell me I should think of it as a compliment.'

Emerson closed his mouth and rubbed his chin as he considered.

'I guess it seemed like a good idea at the time.'

Cassidy was about to let this go, but then the worrying thought, which he now realized he ought to have worked out before, hit him.

'You've done this before,' he murmured. 'Such as when you first worked for this friend of Bret Sanborn. All across the state, I bet, you've been hired to do dubious jobs then chased after rancher's daughters, and all in my name.'

Emerson glanced away to look down at the ranch, laughing.

'Stop taking it so badly. Think of it as building you up a reputation that's a bit more exciting than the one you've got elsewhere.'

'I've got a great reputation with the people I respect,' Cassidy shouted, now feeling the anger he'd suppressed for so long rising up inside. He bunched his fists. 'But I sure as hell don't want ever to find myself riding into a new town again and being arrested for something you've done in my name. What else have you done?'

'Where do you want me to start?' Emerson offered a shamefaced grin, his light tone encouraging Cassidy to view this in a humorous way that Cassidy could never do.

'Take it from the beginning,' he muttered through gritted teeth. 'From the moment you rode off leaving Lorna.'

Emerson closed his eyes, shaking his head.

'I wondered how long it'd be before you mentioned that.'

'Of course I'd mention that,' Cassidy roared. 'She was the woman I loved and you took her away from me.'

Emerson raised a finger. 'Actually, I left her with you.'

Cassidy considered the finger with his fists opening and closing, fighting down an irrational desire to break that finger.

'And what life could we have after you'd been with her?'

Emerson shrugged, as if he'd never considered that Cassidy would take this matter so seriously.

'She was only a woman, and there's heaps of them around. You can find another, and another, and another.' Emerson lightly punched Cassidy's arm and winked. 'Or if you can't, your elder brother can give you some tips.'

Cassidy batted the hand away and leapt to his feet to loom over Emerson.

'Tips are the one thing I don't need from you.'

Emerson flinched back and considered Cassidy's belligerent stance with a smile still on his lips, which only went to annoy Cassidy even more.

'You need plenty.' He slowly got to his feet and stood square on to Cassidy. 'And here's one to start with — stop taking everything so seriously or you'll never learn how to enjoy yourself.'

'You will never tell me what to do!'

Cassidy stopped fighting down the

overwhelming desire to hit Emerson that he'd had ever since he'd seen him at the ranch. He thrust his head down and charged him. He hit him full in the chest and carried him back several paces towards the edge of the ridge before Emerson jabbed in a heel and stopped them moving. Then Emerson pivoted, hurling Cassidy over his side to land beyond the edge.

Cassidy rolled twice before he could stop himself and he came to rest lying on his belly, looking up the slope. He fought to catch his breath but still found that his anger was strengthening by the moment, not receding.

Above him, Emerson stood against the night skyline, his features cast in shadow from the light of the moon behind him, but Cassidy saw him give a barely noticeable beckoning gesture with his hands. Cassidy took him up on his offer.

He jumped to his feet and scrambled up the slope, but at the last moment he veered to the side and gained the top several feet to Emerson's side, then as Emerson lunged for him, he went to one knee.

Emerson's lunging grasp closed on air above his head and with Emerson looming over him, Cassidy leapt to his feet, driving his shoulder up into Emerson's guts and blasting all the air from his chest with a great gasp. Then he bodily lifted him off his feet and hurled him over his shoulder.

Emerson somersaulted in the air before he landed flat on his back. Cassidy didn't give him time to regain his breath and threw himself on him. Then they fought, not in the way Cassidy had dreamed of ten years ago with him pummelling Emerson's face with punch after punch until he could assuage his anger, but like the children they had once been.

With their bodies entangled they rolled one way then the other, flailing and kicking and punching and gouging, the rocks on which they wrestled inflicting more damage to their knees and shoulders than their punches. But eventually they happened to drag themselves clear of each other and both men stood facing each other with their hands held forward and with the bodies hunched forward at the belly.

'Feel better for that?' Emerson said, rolling his shoulders and wincing.

'Not yet,' Cassidy grunted. 'I've only just started on you.'

'Then it's time we got to it.'

Emerson was the first to move in and he threw a great scything mow of a punch at Cassidy's head. Cassidy easily ducked under it, the blow whistling over his head. With Emerson exposing his chest, Cassidy delivered a short arm jab into his stomach that had Emerson bleating in pain, then an uppercut to his chin that stood him straight.

Emerson teetered round on the spot, his arms wheeling, and with him being temporarily winded Cassidy waited for the right moment. And when Emerson staggered round to face him, he threw his entire strength into his own haymaking punch.

Unlike Emerson's previous effort this punch hit its target and sent Emerson wheeling to the dirt where he rolled three times before he came to a halt.

He lay, his chin to the dirt and his back slightly hunched before he flinched, then twisted round to sit looking up at Cassidy.

'Now do you feel better?' he asked, then flexed his jaw.

Cassidy had to admit he did feel a whole lot better, and he allowed himself a short nod while wringing his jarred hand.

'You've had that coming to you for a long time.'

'I guess I did.' Emerson opened his jaw to its utmost then moved his chin from side to side, wincing. He closed it and held his hands wide. 'Is this over now?'

Cassidy reckoned it'd take a dozen more haymaking punches before he'd repaid Emerson for a fraction of the pain he'd caused him ten years ago, and even for the problems he'd caused him recently, but he shrugged.

'I guess if that didn't knock sense into you, nothing ever will.'

'Good,' Emerson said, getting to his feet. 'I'm glad I let you beat me.'

'Let me beat you! You ain't ever let me win at anything before. I beat you.' Cassidy rolled his shoulders and advanced on Emerson, his anger returning with twice the power as before and with an irrational desire to pound Emerson into the dirt for the rest of night overcoming him. 'And I'm going to keep on beating you until you admit that.'

'You can try,' Emerson grunted, beckoning Cassidy on with a small gesture again.

'You won't,' a voice shouted from their side.

'What the . . . ?' Cassidy murmured, stopping and swirling round towards the direction of the speaker. At first he saw nobody, but then Bret stepped out of the shadow of a huge boulder with the glowering Chalk at his side.

'Now,' Bret said, 'we'll take our turn to beat that man to a pulp.'

'Yeah,' Chalk said with undisguised relish, 'and when we've finished, all we'll have left to do is to feed his ugly carcass to the buzzards.'

9

'So this story is the greatest this town's ever known?' Henry said, looking up from his desk to consider Nick. 'That's quite a claim. You'd better get yourself a glass, pour us both a whiskey, and tell me all about it.'

And so Nick did.

Throughout the early part of his tale in which Nick related how Tex had paid him money and how he had decided to enter the hotel, Henry remained stony-faced. But when he reached the denouement, Henry flinched and twitched so hard, Nick thought he might be having a heart attack.

It required two refills of whiskey before Henry regained sufficient composure to quiz Nick and confirm the details, but Nick stuck resolutely to his story and Henry couldn't get him to admit to even an iota of doubt.

The woman he had seen locked in a room in Tex's hotel was Katherine Glover, the woman Luther Manson had kidnapped and Sheriff McGill was searching for, and the woman Tex Beatty claimed he was desperate to find.

There was only one possible explanation. Tex was behind her kidnapping. Although the reason why he had done it, and the issue of whether it confirmed that Tex was responsible for James's murder, eluded Nick.

Henry wended his way past Nick and stood before the window looking down the road at the hotel and at the room with a light on where Katherine was now imprisoned.

Nick had told Henry everything and now he could only wait for him to make his decision. And Nick's entire faith in Henry relied on that decision. If he accepted the story and agreed to print it, he was a man of integrity. If he didn't, he was just another worthless man in Tex's pay.

'Sheriff McGill's not in town, is he?' Henry murmured at last.

'He isn't, just those deputies Lomax and Kendrick, and telling them won't help Katherine none.'

'Whatever your view of them, the law should normally deal with matters like this.'

'They should,' Nick said, 'or if they're not available, people of good faith should try to free her themselves, using guns or force of numbers. But we're newspaper men and our way is the printed word.'

Despite his burst of righteous anger, Nick decided that if Henry dismissed the story, he would seek out Sheriff Cassidy Yates and tell him what he'd seen, but he hoped Henry wouldn't make him do that.

Presently, Henry's shoulders slumped. He turned to face Nick, his lips downturned and his eyes looking at a spot just before Nick's feet. No longer did he look as if he were a man in control. He was a defeated man bowed by a

170

responsibility he never wanted to face, and Nick was sure he was about to disappoint him.

'Nick,' Henry said, his voice barely audible. 'Help me get this story down. Then go to the saloon and get me a bottle of whiskey. This is going to be a long, long night.'

Nick felt such a surge of pride well up from his chest that he thought he was about to be sick. But then Henry bustled into action so quickly that he didn't get the chance to reflect on what he'd achieved and what Henry had agreed to do.

An hour later the report was written and an hour after that, the first page had been typeset. Henry cranked out a printed copy and together they stood over it, reading the details of tomorrow's special issue.

Henry declared himself satisfied, and as the issue included every aspect of the story Nick had uncovered, and didn't attempt to mask Tex's role in Katherine Glover's kidnapping, it satisfied him too. So, feeling more confident now, Nick suggested that with a story of this magnitude, they could go to two pages and charge twice as much.

In response Henry clapped him on the back then heaped so much praise on him, and even explained some of the rudiments of operating the linotype machine, that Nick reckoned his own heart might burst with happiness.

Tonight he had become a newspaper man, he reckoned. For the first time he was doing what he'd always dreamed of doing: reporting the truth and presenting it to the people in a manner which would change their outlook on life.

While Henry set about typesetting the second page, Nick hurried out to the saloon before it closed to fetch Henry his bottle of whiskey.

'Whiskey,' Nick said, leaning on the bar, unable to stop himself smiling.

The bartender eyed him and returned his jovial smile.

'First time, kid?'

'It wouldn't be, but the whiskey's not

for me. It's for Henry Sinclair.'

'Ah, so that would be a bottle. I'll mark it up.'

While the bartender headed away to fetch a bottle, Nick turned and leaned back against the bar. The combination of the townsfolk thronging inside Tex's hotel for his celebration and the lateness of the hour meant that few people were in.

With nothing interesting to catch his eye, Nick looked outside and down the road. His gaze fell on the hotel and he couldn't help but gloat quietly to himself. Tex might be celebrating tonight, but come the morning everyone in town would have to face up to the truth of what this man had been doing. What would happen then, Nick didn't know, but as he was now a newspaper man that wasn't his concern — although he would report on whatever did happen.

A smile twitched at the corner of his mouth as he envisaged the stream of stories his investigative work would create over the coming weeks, but then that smile froze. The *Chronicle* office door was swinging open. Then someone headed inside.

He edged down the bar but he only saw the door close, so he couldn't identify the man who had entered, although from closer to the window, he noticed that the door to Tex's hotel was also open. Despite his glimpse of the person being only fleeting, his movement suggested he'd come from down the road, having stayed in the shadows after leaving Tex's hotel.

With his heightened sense of concern on anything related to Tex Beatty and his hotel, this sight sent a tremor of worry fluttering in Nick's stomach. He swirled round on the spot, eager now to be served so he could get back to the office. Unfortunately, an opportunity to chat with another customer had distracted the bartender. Even when Nick waved an arm and shouted, he couldn't get his attention.

He gave up on fetching the whiskey

bottle and headed to the door.

'Hey,' the bartender shouted. 'What about your whiskey?'

Nick stood in the doorway, looking over the batwings. The office door was still closed, and the hotel door had now closed. Nick told himself to stop worrying then turned.

'Just hurry up,' he grumbled.

'All right, all right,' the bartender said. 'First time in a saloon and already you're complaining.'

Still, the bartender took an inordinate amount of time to find a bottle and place it on the bar. Nick almost gave up on waiting twice more before he had the bottle in hand and could hurry to the door.

Outside, he forced himself to avoid running and paced into the road, again telling himself that he had no need to be concerned.

Then the sudden appearance of a chink of light from down the road caught his attention and stopped him dead in his tracks. The curtain had moved in the hotel room in which Katherine was imprisoned and he glimpsed her form looking down into the road and towards the *Chronicle* office before she slipped back behind the curtain.

Why she'd done this he didn't know, but his heart was now hammering with concern and he speeded his walking. He was half-way across the road when the *Chronicle* office door opened. A man emerged and looked up and down the road, his form shrouded in the shadows and unrecognizable to Nick, although he was too slim to be Henry. His movement stopped with him looking at Nick. Then he thrust his collar up high and headed down the road towards the hotel.

Nick veered away to follow him, his gaze boring into his back as he tried to discern who it was. He had the same build as Tex had, but then again so did Lomax, and for that matter so did many people in Eagle Heights.

Nick drew level with the office

without getting any clearer idea as to who he was, but the man was approaching the hotel where he would be bathed in light as he entered. Then he would be able to see him properly.

But another chink of light caught his gaze, and this time it was flickering and coming from the *Chronicle* office.

Nick darted his gaze to the side, and what he saw shocked him so much he almost fell to his knees. He stared for long moments, his mind not registering what he was seeing.

Only when he saw the first tendril of smoke snake out through the door did he react.

He broke into a run, looking sideways as he ran, but the man had slipped into the hotel while he'd been distracted. He put that matter from his mind and hurried the rest of the way across the road.

He threw open the door, taking in the scene of the broken furniture, the strewn paper, Henry lying sprawled over his linotype machine before his gaze returned to what had shocked him. Then he turned and took two long paces to stand on the edge of the boardwalk.

'Fire,' he shouted at the top of his lungs. 'Fire! Fire!'

★　★　★

'I've waited a long time for this,' Chalk said, pacing past Bret. He unhooked his gunbelt and threw it on to the looping pile of weaponry containing Cassidy's and Emerson's confiscated guns.

Cassidy noted the positioning of those guns in case he needed to make a run for them, but despite Bret's and Chalk's bravado and bluster, he hoped he wouldn't have to make that attempt. And after his recent burst of anger, Cassidy appreciated why Chalk wanted to pummel Emerson into the dirt.

Standing on the edge of the ridge, he kept his expression calm and his stance unthreatening as Chalk glared at

Emerson then shouted out his oath-filled opinion of him. In the occasional break in Chalk's ranting, Bret offered his own low opinion of Emerson and shouted encouragement to Chalk.

For his part Emerson took Chalk's complaints with barely a flicker in his smile and when he gave that barely noticeable beckoning-on gesture that had so annoyed Cassidy, Chalk moved in.

Bret shot Cassidy a warning glance that ordered him not to intervene. Cassidy nodded, then returned to watching the two men.

Chalk had worked himself up so much that his first punches were berserk and flailing and, despite the battering he'd received from Cassidy, Emerson avoided them easily. Then Emerson moved in and shoved Chalk, at the same time looping a foot around his ankle. Chalk fell all his length on his back and lay for a moment, cursing.

Emerson paced around him, uncon-cerned, and with Bret urging him on,

Chalk rolled to his knees, then keeping low surged to his feet and charged Emerson. Again acting casually, Emerson danced aside to let Chalk stomp on by and even aimed a contemptuous kick at his receding back, which missed. Then with his arms folded he swung round to watch Chalk slide to a halt.

Chalk turned on his heel, his face suffused to blackness in the gloom, and advanced on Emerson, but after his initial efforts had failed, a certain amount of sense descended on him. He moved in deliberately, his fists raised, and Emerson must have detected the change in Chalk's attitude because his smile faded and he stood tall before him, even backing away and wheeling round as he kept him in view.

The two men circled, their gazes locked on each other.

Chalk was the first to try an offensive move and he stomped in, then jabbed a punch at Emerson's head. Again Emerson swayed away easily, but this time the punch was a feint as was

Chalk's second blow and his third.

Cassidy saw a flash of doubt cloud Emerson's eyes as he wondered what Chalk's tactics were. Chalk moved in again, aiming another series of punches at Emerson's head, and again they were all feints that dropped some way short of their possible target.

Emerson muttered to himself, then decided to get the fight under way. He paced in, his fist arcing round with a forceful punch that surely wouldn't be a feint. But Chalk had achieved what he had wanted to do by goading Emerson into acting without care and he danced to the side lightly in a way he hadn't done so far, then came at Emerson from the side. He punched him in the ear, rocking his head to the side, then swung up his left fist into his chin, standing him upright.

Then Chalk delivered a flurry of fast and determined punches into Emerson's body and face that rocked him back and forth. No matter which direction he went, Chalk was there to hit him and every retaliatory punch Emerson aimed at Chalk fell short.

Chalk's domination of the brawl was so great that Cassidy slowly nodded to himself, deciding that Emerson had seen sense and was letting Chalk work off his anger on him to preserve his life. But to achieve that aim would require him to prevail through a lot more battering. Despite his previous anger, Cassidy wished him luck — and for Chalk to tire quickly.

For the next two minutes Chalk continued to hit him but the gaps between his punches lengthened. Chalk must have accepted that he was tiring because he rolled his shoulders, summoning his strength, and delivered a pile-driver of a punch that knocked Emerson's feet clear off the ground and wheeled him away. He rolled twice before slamming into Cassidy's shins, halting him.

Cassidy knelt to give him an encouraging pat on the back.

'Stay down,' he whispered. 'That

could be enough.'

Emerson grunted his low opinion of this suggestion and pushed Cassidy aside as he gained his feet. He stood with his feet planted wide and with his head lolling.

Cassidy didn't think he could withstand much more punishment but he felt a flicker of pride that Emerson was letting Chalk pummel him for so long.

Chalk moved in, using the same confident manner as before to deliver a second round of battering, the short break helping him to bolster his strength.

Emerson stood before him, swaying and darting his gaze around with glazed eyes as if he was so disorientated that he was unable to locate from where his assailant would come. He didn't appear capable of defending himself, and Cassidy reckoned he'd need all his strength just to avoid falling over even without Chalk's help, but when Chalk swung a punch at him, Emerson regained his senses and darted aside.

The punch missed, leaving Chalk with his arm thrust out over Emerson's shoulder.

Cassidy just had time to realize that Emerson had been feigning being more hurt than he was, but that realization was too late for Chalk. Emerson grabbed Chalk's outstretched arm in both hands, one hand clasping his fist and the other the elbow, then yanked down and up, swinging Chalk round to place his back to him.

He twisted, then thrust Chalk's arm so far up his back that Cassidy winced expecting to hear bones crack, but Chalk just avoided that by going up on tiptoes. With him off-balance Emerson shoved, forcing Chalk to his knees. After that, the fight was over in a matter of moments as, with grim efficiency, Emerson released Chalk's arm, grabbed the back of his head and thrust down, slamming Chalk's head into the solid rock below.

Chalk slumped to lie on his front without uttering a sound, leaving

Emerson to stand batting his hands together. He didn't even check that he had knocked out his assailant and instead turned to face Bret, a contented smile on his face. Bret considered the comatose Chalk, then ordered Emerson to join Cassidy.

Emerson headed over to Cassidy with a slight swagger in his gait, while Bret checked on Chalk. He rolled him over and slapped his cheeks several times before he received a murmured and disorientated oath.

'I told you,' Cassidy said, leaning closer to Emerson, 'that you could never let another man beat you.'

'And you were right,' Emerson said proudly, 'as always.'

'Trouble is, I reckon Bret is about to make you pay for that mistake.'

This comment made Emerson wince, and sure enough, when Bret had convinced himself that Chalk would be fine, he directed both men to lie on the ground, face down. He tied them up, securing their hands and their feet.

Then he dragged them away from the edge of the ridge and placed them with their backs to a boulder and facing away from the ridge.

By the time he'd completed his task, Chalk was sitting up and looking at them, his eyes unfocused and pained, but in them the desire for revenge burned stronger than ever.

'Get to it then,' Emerson demanded as Bret stood back from him.

'There's no hurry,' Bret said. 'I want to savour this.'

'Me too,' Chalk said, his voice shaking. He got to his feet, swayed before he could get his balance, then wended over to Emerson, where he hunkered down before him so he could share his eye-line. 'And you can savour wondering what I'm about to do to you.'

'You ain't got the imagination to do anything interesting,' Emerson said, 'or at least that's what Annie said.'

Chalk snorted his breath and rocked forward, his fist rising, but then got his anger under control and stood. He paced away to stand on the edge of the ridge and look down to the ranch, a shaking hand probing his forehead.

Emerson turned his head to watch him leave, a smile on his face as he probably searched for more ways to taunt his captor.

Cassidy ignored his unhelpful brother and instead looked up at Bret, who was also watching Chalk, concern narrowing his eyes.

'Well,' Cassidy said, 'now you've got us all tied up, what are you going to do with a lawman and a mere suspect?'

'You know what I plan to do.'

'I do, but I also know you're having second thoughts. Back away from this while you still can. You could ruin any chance of getting justice for your friend James Glover. Emerson didn't kill him, but he might hold the key to proving Tex Beatty did.'

Bret flinched, swirling round to stare down at him.

'Tex Beatty didn't . . . ' He looked

away. 'But then again, I guess he could have . . . '

'See, you have your doubts, and you've got to give me the time to work all this out. And no matter what I discover, one thing is certain — Emerson was with Annie on the night James died and — '

'And that just brings us round to the other problem,' Bret roared, the sudden possibility that he might be prepared to act reasonably disappearing as quickly as it had come. 'Either he wasn't with my daughter and he killed James, or he was and he's just as guilty.'

'Listen to what you're saying. Chalk and Emerson have just fought out their problems and that should be the end of it.' Cassidy paused when Chalk grunted that this wasn't the case, then continued: 'Now, it has to be up to Annie to decide what she wants to do about Emerson.'

'It is not,' Bret roared but as his statement echoed back to him, another voice spoke up from the edge of the ridge.

'But it is my decision.'

Everyone looked around to see who had spoken, and Cassidy's gaze quickly alighted on Annie. She had a basket looped over an arm as she picked her way over the edge of the ridge, some twenty yards to Chalk's side.

'Annie, how did . . . ?' Bret sighed then pointed a firm finger at her. 'Stay away from this.'

'You were making enough noise to be heard in Eagle Heights,' she said, still walking towards them. 'And I will have my say.'

Bret firmed his jaw and Cassidy thought he was about to refuse, but he nodded.

'You are my daughter and as strong-willed as any son I might have had,' he said proudly. 'You can have your say, but I will also do what I must.'

Annie nodded, then continued walking until she stood before Emerson. She set the basket down and removed a steaming coffee-pot wrapped in a towel, then unwrapped the towel and laid a hunk of bread and salted beef-strips on it, possibly prolonging the moment before she had to look at Emerson.

Then she looked at him.

Long moments passed in which Cassidy hoped she would be able to provide a reasonable and calming argument that would veer Bret and Chalk away from the disastrous course they were determined to follow. But a moment before she reacted Cassidy saw the sudden flaring in her eyes and realized that that wouldn't happen. Emerson must have seen it too because he flinched away, but he reacted too slowly.

She hurled herself at him, a furious combination of feet and clawed hands raking at him. She delivered two stinging slaps to his cheek that rocked his head one way then the other, then a swinging kick to his belly that tumbled him on his back. In self-preservation Emerson rolled on to his side and hunched his legs up to his chin. Still she flailed at him, slapping his back and kicking him in the side.

Bret eventually reacted and darted in. He grabbed her around the waist and tried to drag her away but she was acting as if possessed. Her arms and legs flailed as she hit Emerson again, delivering several painful blows to his body before Bret was able to move her away.

Only when Emerson was well out of her range did she collapse to slump in his grasp.

'I've finished with him,' she declared, her voice defeated, these the only words she'd uttered during her assault.

Bret held on to her for a few moments longer, giving her a fatherly squeeze of approval and sympathy, then led her away so that she didn't need to see Emerson any more.

'I'll walk you back to the ranch,' he said, releasing her.

'No,' she said, regaining her composure with a patting of her hair and a smoothing of the crinkles from her dress. 'The cold air will do me some good. Just drink the coffee and enjoy the food, then do with him as you will.'

Having given that permission, she raised her chin and left, leaving no time for argument. Bret watched her go with considerable pride and concern in his gaze then paced back to stand before Emerson and Cassidy.

Chalk joined him and now, after Annie's outburst, Cassidy saw no possibility of mercy in either of their cold gazes.

'Bret,' Cassidy said, speaking quickly before the men went too far, beyond the point of no return. 'We all want to know who killed James Glover and killing us won't help you uncover that. Think long and hard before you do anything.'

Bret nodded then knelt beside the basket Annie had left. He felt the coffee-pot.

'And I intend to,' he said. He grinned without humour, and in the moonlight his face was a mask of death. 'We'll enjoy a warming drink and some food while we work out exactly what we'll do to you.'

'And,' Chalk said, joining Bret, 'exactly where we can bury your bodies.'

Then Bret and Chalk got to work on consuming the coffee and food that Annie had brought. Despite their comments neither man spoke, devoting their time to glaring at Emerson. Both men put the food into their mouths and slurped their coffee with the grim determination of people who refused to enjoy what they were eating in case it distracted them from the more important task at hand.

Cassidy glanced at Emerson, who was still lying in the position he'd assumed to avoid Annie's anger. His cheek lay on the ground and he appeared to have retreated inside himself, focusing his eyes on a spot a few inches from his nose.

Cassidy wanted to ask him why

Annie had attacked him, as it contradicted everything he thought he knew about Annie's opinion of their relationship. But in the circumstances he didn't want to give Bret and Chalk any encouragement to begin acting out their revenge.

As it was, they were ready soon enough.

Bret issued Chalk with brisk instructions to look down the side of the ridge and confirm that Annie had now reached the ranch. Chalk did as ordered and hurried to the edge of the ridge, then took a few paces down it as he peered into the gloom, leaving Bret to glare down at Emerson.

'You ready to beg for your life?' Bret asked, presently.

He didn't get a response and he asked his question again. Still he didn't get an answer, and so he looked to the side, beckoning Chalk in with a sharp gesture. Then he flinched and narrowed his eyes.

Cassidy followed his gaze to see that

Chalk was no longer standing just beyond the ridge.

With his brow furrowed, Bret took a single pace towards the last place he'd seen him, but then his foot slipped and his leg gave way to tumble him to his knees. A hand shot up to rub his forehead.

'What the . . . ?' Bret murmured. Then like a felled tree he tumbled forward to lie with his face pressed into the dirt.

Cassidy echoed Bret's plea with his own bemused comment, but it was Emerson who provided an answer as he rolled up to a sitting position, then shuffled round to place his back to him.

'Stop asking stupid questions,' he said, 'and get over here. I don't want to slash my wrists cutting through the ropes with this here knife.'

'This here . . . '

Cassidy nodded with sudden understanding as he saw the knife that Emerson had been concealing behind his back. Annie had drugged Bret and

Chalk with the food and coffee and her assault had just been a cover for her giving him the knife.

Cassidy didn't waste time on clarifying this and in short order both men were slicing through their bonds. As Emerson peeled away the last of the ropes, Annie appeared. She ran over the edge of the ridge and across the top then threw herself into his arms.

'I did it,' she said.

'And you did well,' Emerson said, drawing her away from him and smiling.

She fingered a scrape on his cheek. 'Did I hurt you?'

'You could never hurt me.'

'Then did *he* hurt you?'

'That was even more unlikely.'

Cassidy gave them a few moments together, enjoying seeing that despite Emerson's earlier unsubtle comments, he did look at her and treat her with affection.

Presently he coughed, drawing their attention to him.

'I have to go now,' he said. 'I've got to arrest Tex Beatty.'

'I'm coming with you,' Emerson said, extricating himself from Annie's arms.

'No need. Stay here and enjoy Annie's company.'

Emerson's eyes flashed with more concern than he'd shown throughout the last few perilous hours.

'You need me,' he urged. 'The only proof I uncovered of what Tex did was the contract that cut James out of their business partnership. I know where another copy will be.'

Although Cassidy would have preferred to act without Emerson's help, he had to admit he could do with some aid and he nodded. Emerson moved to follow him, but Annie danced forward and looped an arm around his waist.

'I'm coming with you,' she said.

'You can't,' Emerson said. 'This could get mighty dangerous.'

'I don't care. I'm never, ever letting you out of my sight again.' She threw her arms around his neck and clung on with a limpetlike hold that really did look as if she'd never release him.

Emerson patted her back as with beseeching eyes he looked over her shoulder at Cassidy.

Cassidy was minded to ignore Emerson's request, but Annie's presence was a complication they didn't need.

'You can't come, Annie,' he said. He glanced at Bret's unconscious body. 'Your father and Chalk will come to soon and if you and Emerson are ever going to be able to start that life together, you need to stop them from coming after us.'

'How?' she asked, peeling away from Emerson.

Cassidy shrugged. 'Bret's your kin, so that's for you to decide, but at the very least you've got to explain away what happened, then send them off in the opposite direction to Eagle Heights.'

Annie nodded, then turned to Emerson. 'And you'll come back to me as soon as you possibly can?'

'Of course,' Emerson said, pointing to the high moon, 'with the moon at my back as I promised.'

'And I'll wait for you,' Annie said.

She planted a huge kiss on his cheek and gave him a desperate rib-crunching hug. Then with a barely suppressed sob she backed away and set about dragging Chalk's body closer to Bret's leaving Emerson and Cassidy to head off to Eagle Heights.

They were out of Annie's hearing range when Emerson turned to Cassidy and shook his head, sighing.

'You just had to come up with that excuse, didn't you?'

'Only because you weren't planning on telling her the truth that you'll never come back, were you?'

'Sure right I wasn't. But better that than the lie you told her.'

'I figured my lie might give you time to think and so it might not have to be a lie.' Cassidy glanced back towards the ridge. 'That Annie would be feisty enough to do you some good.'

'That's what my younger brother reckons, is it?'

'Yup. And once I've arrested Tex Beatty, I reckon I'll start work on persuading my older brother to listen to me.'

Emerson opened his mouth, probably to state that this wouldn't work, but for once he closed it without a retort.

10

Henry Sinclair was dead.

Enough people had hurried out of the saloon and even Tex's hotel, although Nick would have preferred not to have had these people's help, to avert the potential disaster.

The fire had been only a small one, consuming just Nick's and Henry's notes and the printed copy of the special issue. But what the man who had entered the office had then done had ensured that Henry wouldn't be the one who could reveal the contents of that special issue.

Henry's mouth was brimming with ashes, his bright red face, and his bulging eyes suggesting the man had crammed the burnt paper down his throat until he'd choked.

A gaggle of people had dragged Henry out into the road, but they'd been unable to revive him and now they'd gathered around him with their heads lowered. Presently the deputies Lomax and Kendrick arrived from Tex's hotel.

Nick backed away to stand on the boardwalk where he could watch them, noting again that the man who had entered the office earlier had the same build as Lomax had. Both men glanced his way before embarking on a round of questioning. They received the story that Nick had alerted them and so they'd dragged Henry outside while others extinguished the fire. Neither man looked Nick's way for corroboration and Nick stayed where he was.

Nick gradually accepted that fear as to what the deputies might do to him was rooting him to the spot. But he also vowed that he wouldn't let the person who had killed Henry get away with it. He waited for the right moment to blurt out what he knew.

Despite several people looking Nick's way while they explained what had happened, neither deputy called him over. When everyone had had their say both men stood back from the body.

'Henry clearly had a heart attack,' Kendrick declared. 'He did have a weak heart.'

'I agree,' said Lomax, 'and he must have been smoking when it happened and that started the fire.'

Silence reigned for several seconds until someone who, from the way he slurred his words, was so much the worse for drink that he was unable to care whom he annoyed, asked, 'Then why was all that ash in his mouth?'

Lomax shot this man a warning glare, then turned to face Nick for the first time. He raised his voice for Nick's benefit.

'Only Henry Sinclair could ever answer that, but I believe he accidentally started the fire in a basket of paper. He had a heart attack while trying to put it out and fell over head first into the basket and so the ashes fell into his open mouth.'

While Lomax continued to look at Nick, Kendrick glanced around, defying anyone to contradict this unlikely version of events.

Nick took deep breaths as he gathered his courage to offer his own version, but Lomax's firm gaze assured him that if he were to blurt out what he suspected, he would be dead before he completed that accusation. And Nick had no doubt that somehow the deputies would then find a way to explain away why they'd killed him, and that nobody would question them. Then Tex Beatty would be free to do as he pleased, and Katherine Glover would remain a prisoner in his hotel.

Nick darted his gaze at each of the bystanders, wondering if any of them would come to his aid if he did speak up. But everyone was either someone who'd emerged from the saloon or someone who had come from Tex's hotel and Nick didn't reckon either of these groups would have the courage or the willingness to help him. Worse, even that small possibility disappeared when everyone began to peel away from Henry's body to return to doing what they'd been doing before.

While the deputies stayed to stare at Nick, two people stayed back to move Henry's body. Nick watched the bystanders spread out, then decided to follow Henry's body. He headed off the boardwalk, but Lomax moved sideways blocking his path.

'Where you going, Nick?' he demanded.

Nick glanced past Lomax to see that Kendrick had moved round to block his way to the saloon. The bystanders were now all closing on their destinations and only the two men who were manoeuvring Henry's body were nearby, but they were already half-way across the road and weren't paying attention to this confrontation.

Despite the desperate situation, Nick gathered up his courage and looked Lomax in the eye.

'I just want to honour my friend's memory, and maybe later I might drink to him in the saloon.' Nick considered his comment and reckoned Lomax might view it as confrontational, so he ended with what he hoped would be a useful reminder of what bound them, even if he didn't believe it. 'I could even spend the money Tex gave me.'

'I'd keep it. After what you've done, Tex won't be paying you no more.' Lomax laughed, the sound grating and hollow. 'Although you could be right. After what you did you might as well spend that money real quick.'

'If that's a threat,' Nick said, throwing off all pretence of finding common ground with Lomax, 'I've got one of my own, and you know what it is.'

Lomax let his mouth drop open in a parody of fear. He glanced at Kendrick so he could share his amusement, but Nick had received the reaction he wanted and with Lomax distracted, he moved to pass by him on his left hand side. Lomax shot out a hand to stop him, but Nick had anticipated his action and he ducked low and side-stepped to pass under his arm on Lomax's right.

Lomax's fleeting grasp closed on his collar, but he shrugged his hand off and continued walking. The men who were carrying Henry's body were now the only other people out on the road, and he followed them. But already they had reached the boardwalk outside the undertaker's. Nick willed them to find that the door was closed so that they'd have to remain outside while the undertaker opened the door, giving him enough time to cross the road. But to his annoyance the door opened, a hand beckoned them in, and the men slipped inside.

Then Nick was alone on the road with Lomax and Kendrick, and there were no witnesses to whatever they decided to do to him. Nick half-expected lead to hammer into his back straight away and his neck itched as he imagined them using him as a target, but he heard only the two men following him.

He still judged that being in the company of others was his safest option, and as he crossed the road he weighed up the benefits of the undertaker's against the saloon. Whichever he chose, he would still have the problem of what he would do when everyone had retired for the night and had left him on his own. Nick shivered and resolved that he wouldn't risk keeping the information he had private a moment longer, no matter what the cost.

That meant he needed the biggest audience possible, and he'd find that in the saloon. He veered to the side on his route across the road, seeing the saloon was just thirty or so paces ahead of him. Nick started counting those paces. He'd reached ten and was entering the square of light cast through the saloon's windows when the steady footfalls behind him speeded.

Nick stopped maintaining the illusion that he was trying to walk away from his pursuers calmly.

He ran for his life.

The footsteps behind him were so close he could imagine that the wind rushing by was Lomax's breath on his neck, and this spurred him on to run as fast as he could. He pounded onto the boardwalk with long strides, then saw the batwings swing open before him. A man appeared looking into the road.

With a surge of delight at having gained a witness, Nick sprinted the last few yards, but then saw that the man wouldn't help him. This man swung his gaze down onto him and flared his eyes, then hunched down with his hands held wide as if to catch a wild hog.

With Lomax and Kendrick closing in different directions from behind Nick had no choice but to try and get into the saloon. He kept running, then hurled himself to the boardwalk. He slid on his belly, aiming to go through the man's legs and under the batwings. And if he'd timed his leap better, he might have succeeded.

His head poked out into the saloon

as he skidded to a halt and he enjoyed a moment where he faced numerous witnesses, but nobody was looking his way. Then he scrambled forward but he was too late. Hands clamped down on his back, dragged him backwards and out of the saloon.

He shouted out a plea for help that didn't rouse any of the customers, then he found himself lying outside on the boardwalk. He twisted, throwing himself on his back and looked up to see Lomax and Kendrick looming over him and grinning. Lomax lunged down to grab his collar, but Nick jerked his head to the side and bit his hand.

Lomax cursed, flinching back and letting Nick see clear space ahead. Nick squirmed and kicked, freeing himself from the man holding him down. On hands and knees he scrambled away down the boardwalk.

He covered a few shuffled feet before a hand clamped down on his back, but Nick bodily threw himself forward and he heard his jacket rip before he tumbled away. He rolled once then came up on his feet and pounded down the boardwalk, concentrating on running as fast as he could, the deputies hurrying after him.

Unfortunately, he put all his efforts into his running and so he headed past the undertaker's — perhaps the only easily attainable place where he could find witnesses. He winced, skidded to a halt and moved to turn back, but already the deputies were running past the undertaker's, now just yards behind him.

Nick turned on his heel and ran, but he'd wasted valuable seconds with his unsuccessful manoeuvre and now the deputies were closing on him with every stride.

He passed a point where he was level with the *Chronicle* office on the other side of the road and carried on to draw level with Tex's hotel, but now Lomax and Kendrick were nipping at his heels. Then Lomax grunted an order for Kendrick to grab him.

Nick didn't give him the chance. He stopped himself dead, turned on his heel, ducked to pass under Kendrick's flailing arm, then ran off again, this time for the only unoccupied space ahead, an alley.

Instantly the light-level dropped and Nick suffered a moment of hollow despair. Out on the road he had at least had the security of potential witnesses, but in the dark the two men were free to do whatever they wanted to do to him. Nick resolved to not give them that chance. He fixed his gaze on the end of the alley and pounded towards it. Behind him, he heard footfalls, but the deputies weren't chasing him as quickly as before, almost as if they knew he couldn't escape this way.

Still, Nick let himself enjoy the hope that he might find sanctuary when he reached the end of the alley, but three-quarters of the way along, all hope disappeared.

A man stepped out into the alley ahead, blocking his exit. It was too dark to see who it was, but the man stood close to one wall, his legs planted wide and his form silhouetted against the sky beyond. A second man paced into the alley to join him, completely blocking the route ahead. Nick slid to a halt and looked around, but the walls on either side of him were solid, without windows or doors.

He looked back to see Lomax and Kendrick slow to a halt behind him, only their outlines visible.

'This is the end, Nick,' Lomax said, his tone hollow and crushing any hope of mercy. 'You could have enjoyed the benefits of working for Tex Beatty, but now you get to enjoy the taste of lead.'

Nick looked left and right, a numb resignation overcoming him as he accepted that there was nothing he could do. In a final act of defiance, he turned his back on Lomax and Kendrick, ensuring they'd have to shoot him in the back, and so maybe giving them a problem later when they tried to explain themselves. He looked down the alley at the other two men. Then one of them spoke. And Nick recognized the voice.

'Drop!' the man said simply.

Nick immediately understood and he hurled himself to the ground as the man whirled his arm, his gun coming to a hand in a moment and blasting lead in twin spurts of fire. Nick had barely hit the ground when he heard the deputies cry out behind him, then heard them thud to the ground.

He still stayed down, only raising his head when the two men ahead moved off down the alley.

'Now, Cassidy,' the man who hadn't fired said, 'where did you learn to shoot like that?'

'Had plenty of time on my hands after you took Lorna away from me.'

'You just won't let this go, will you?'

Cassidy snorted then hunkered down beside Nick.

'You fine, Nick?' he asked.

'I am now,' Nick said.

'Can I assume from what Lomax just

tried to do that you've uncovered yet more useful information?'

Nick nodded. Then he allowed himself a prolonged shake of his whole body and a rapid pacing up and down to free some of the nervous tension that he reckoned might never go away after his brush with death. Then he went on to explain. Both men stayed quiet except when Nick mentioned the room in which Tex had imprisoned Katherine.

'She's in the same room,' Emerson said, 'as the contract that cut James out of their partnership is in.'

'Perhaps Tex likes to keep all his valuables in one place,' Cassidy said.

When Nick had finished explaining, both men headed off down the alley, pausing only to stop and mutter a few words of contempt over the bodies of the deputies. In the main road, Cassidy and Emerson looked at the hotel, and with Nick's help they picked out Katherine's room.

'Nick,' Cassidy said, patting him on the back, 'you've done well, but now you need to stay here where it's safe.'

Nick shook his head. 'I reckon I'll be safer with you.'

Cassidy considered then gave a brief nod. Then with Nick a few paces behind he and Emerson set off across the road.

'What's your plan?' Emerson asked, running his gaze over the hotel.

'The simplest,' Cassidy said. 'We head inside, get Katherine out, then arrest Tex.'

'And I guess if he tries to stop us he gets what those deputies got?'

'That's the way it is.'

Behind them, Nick coughed, drawing their attention to him.

'You could use the window up there.' He pointed, tracing out the route he'd used earlier from the hotel next door then across the balconies to the upstairs window.

Cassidy shook his head. 'I'm going in as the law and that means I don't sneak in through windows.'

'A pity,' Emerson said as they

216

reached the boardwalk. 'I reckon I'm better at sneaking in through windows than heading in through front doors.'

Cassidy snorted. 'If you were any good at sneaking in through windows, you wouldn't be in the mess you're in now.'

Cassidy set off as Emerson murmured a resigned agreement. Then all three men headed inside. They looked neither left nor right at the various people milling around downstairs, as they headed straight for the stairs then hurried up them.

Nick kept pace with Cassidy and Emerson, gathering that neither man wanted to give anyone a chance to waylay them. He caught a fleeting glimpse of Tex amongst the crowd and heard several complaints rise up from various quarters, demanding to know what they were doing, but that didn't slow them. When they reached the top of the stairs, Nick pointed out the room in which Katherine was imprisoned.

Cassidy went straight to the door and knocked.

'Ma'am,' he said, 'this is Sheriff Cassidy Yates and I don't want you to be alarmed but I'm coming in.'

Cassidy didn't wait for a response. He took a step backwards, then kicked the door by the lock. He required three firm kicks before the door splintered away from the frame. Then he strode inside.

All three men paced inside to find Katherine standing by the bed, a hastily removed blanket clutched to her chin.

'Take one step towards me and I scream,' she warned with calm assurance.

'That's fine with me,' Cassidy said. 'The more people who know you're here the better, but you've got no reason to be frightened. You're not a prisoner no more.'

'But I'm not a prisoner now,' she said, her tone sounding aghast at the thought. 'Tex is protecting me.'

'Protecting you?' Cassidy intoned, incredulous.

'As James would have done if he were still alive.' Katherine continued to look at Cassidy as he shook his head in bemusement and she acknowledged how unlikely this sounded with a slight smile. 'It is a mite unconventional, I admit, but so is Tex.'

'Unconventional ain't the word I'd use to describe having a bandit kidnap you.'

Katherine's mouth fell open in shock. In the pause Nick heard footsteps pounding up the stairs. Then Tex's unmistakable arrogant tones echoed as he issued orders for everyone to be calm and to let him deal with the situation.

Cassidy swung round to face the open door with his gun drawn while Emerson glanced around the room until his gaze fell on a safe by the wall. He hurried over to it, confirmed it was locked, then hunkered down before it and fingered around the sides of the door as if he had the necessary skill to break in. But even if he had, Nick didn't reckon he'd get enough time as Tex and his cohorts stomped to a halt just outside the door.

'You men in there,' Tex demanded, 'lay one finger on her and you'll be a long time regretting it.'

Cassidy glanced at Nick, then at Emerson and put a finger to his lips. Emerson barely glanced at him as his fingers whirled the lock, trying to crack the combination.

'I note,' Cassidy said, speaking slowly, presumably to give Emerson more time to get into the safe, 'that you didn't reveal the name of the person in here, but I'm prepared to do that. Katherine Glover won't be your prisoner no longer and when everyone knows what you've done, you'll lose all those people you reckon are your friends.'

A murmuring at the mentioning of her name went up in the corridor and to drown it out, Tex spoke quickly and loudly.

'I won't. There is no prisoner in there.'

Katherine murmured her agreement of this, causing Cassidy to furrow his brow.

'How can you say that when I'm standing right next to Katherine?'

Outside in the corridor, Tex didn't reply immediately. In the silence Nick wondered how he would seek to explain away what he'd done, but when it came, it rocked all three men inside back on their heels.

'Because it's true,' Tex said, his tone now sad and defeated. 'I had no choice but to keep Katherine safe in there until I was sure that Luther Manson was long gone. You see, I paid the ransom to free her.'

★ ★ ★

Cassidy leaned back against the wall outside the office of the Eagle Heights *Chronicle*. Nick was at his side, looking into the office, but as yet he hadn't been able to persuade himself to go in.

It was mid-afternoon. Two hours

earlier Sheriff McGill had returned to town and although he had still to find Luther Manson, he reacted to the news that he didn't need to search for Katherine Glover with the suspicion Cassidy had expected.

For most of the next two hours McGill had quizzed Tex Beatty in the sheriff's office. Only now had Tex emerged to stand outside, his face pale and his shoulders hunched. Emerson had gone in to the sheriff's office to explain his own actions, and in his case Cassidy wished him well.

'You've got to go into the newspaper office sometime, Nick,' Cassidy said, turning away from his consideration of Tex.

'I know,' Nick said, 'but now that Henry's dead I'm not sure whether there is a newspaper.'

'Town this size always needs a newspaper, and I can't think of a better person to bring it to the people than you.'

'That still depends on him.' Nick

pointed down the road at Tex, who was now walking towards them. 'And whether he'll let me bring that news to the people.'

Nick shuffled round to stand behind Cassidy as Cassidy turned to face Tex.

'McGill accept your explanation?' he asked.

'He did,' Tex said, 'eventually.'

Cassidy nodded. 'And what was it?'

'The same as I told you last night. Jackson Dyer brought me Luther Manson's ransom demand. I paid the messenger — not that it did Jackson any good — then paid Luther. If I had involved McGill, Luther would have killed her, so I hid Katherine and put the sheriff off the trail to give Luther enough time to get away, as per our agreement.'

'And McGill accepted that?'

'He wasn't happy, as I guess you aren't, but you and he are now free to go after him without the worry that Katherine could die. That was my only concern and if I found myself in the same situation again, I would act in exactly the same way.'

Cassidy rubbed his jaw as he considered this tale, finding in it the ring of truth, except for one detail.

'Why did Luther Manson just happen to kidnap her in the first place?'

'James was in dire financial trouble. He owed people money everywhere. I guess one of those creditors might have been behind it.'

'If James was in that much trouble, it sure was a pity for him that you planned to drive him out of your business partnership.'

Tex narrowed his eyes at this accusing comment, but then shrugged.

'I didn't cause his troubles by cutting him out of our partnership. I cut him out *because* of his financial troubles. He was bringing both of us down.'

Cassidy nodded slowly, raising his eyebrows.

'I guess you're right. Financial troubles could have been plenty motivation for someone to kill him.'

'I reckon they were,' Tex said, neutrally, not rising to the bait. Then he nudged to the side to look at Nick. 'But I don't want to read unsubstantiated allegations about me in my newspaper.'

'Your newspaper?' Nick blurted out, coming out from behind Cassidy.

'Of course. I own this building and everything in it, including Henry's precious linotype machine and anything that might appear in print.'

'I didn't know you owned the *Chronicle*, but that kind of situation sure isn't healthy for those who care about the truth,' Nick grumbled, then glared up at Tex with defiance blazing in his eyes. 'But no matter, a man like you can't avoid the truth for ever.'

Tex considered Nick, and Cassidy saw the faint suspicion of a smile on his lips.

'You sound just like a young Henry Sinclair when he first came to me and asked me to lend him the money to start up the *Chronicle*. I trust you will continue his good work.'

'Not under your terms.'

Tex spread his hands with a benevolent gesture that despite the explanations Cassidy had heard he chose not to believe.

'My terms are simple — report the truth, and there is no truth in what you're alleging. I may have given money to many people but I don't control what they then do. I never told Lomax to kill Jackson Dyer or Henry Sinclair or you.' Tex turned to look at Cassidy. 'And neither did I have anything to do with James's murder. If you want to find out who did it, you'll have to investigate every person whom he owed money to, or who owed him, and that didn't include me.'

Cassidy narrowed his eyes. 'What you mean about owed to him?'

Tex shrugged. 'James was calling in plenty of debts to pay his other creditors and that was causing many people problems. There was Jim Bradley, the bartender, Chalk Pendleton, then there was — '

Cassidy raised a hand, silencing him.

'In truth, this has nothing to do with me. You've explained yourself to Sheriff McGill and it's up to him to complete his investigation of James's murder. The only thing I care about is that my brother is no longer under suspicion, and that Nick gets to run a newspaper his way.'

Both men turned to look at Nick. The young man was looking through the office window and Cassidy could see the desperate desire to go inside in his eyes, but he shook his head and reached into his pocket. He removed two bills from his pocket and held them out to Tex, but when Tex didn't take them he opened his hand and let them drop to the ground.

'I will never take your money,' he said, standing tall with more dignity than Cassidy would have expected in one so young. 'A newspaper man must have integrity. I will clean out the office because Henry wouldn't have wanted me to leave it in any other state. Then I'm leaving to find another town and another newspaper where I am free to be the man I wish to be.'

Nick nodded to Cassidy, shrugged his ripped jacket until it hung smoothly, then headed into the office. With a sad shake of the head, Tex watched him leave then turned to go, but Cassidy stopped him with a cough.

'I've said none of this is my concern, but for me the one thing that doesn't add up here is why you were so desperate to protect James's widow.'

'I am a sympathetic man,' Tex said, looking into the road.

'And I'm sure you took every opportunity the situation afforded to spend time with her and to . . . to let her get to know you better.'

Tex snorted his breath then glanced back at Cassidy, and from his downcast gaze and low voice Cassidy reckoned he was hearing the full truth for the first time.

'I have had feelings for her, I admit that, since long before she even met James, but do not think that that was a reason for me to kill him. He was my friend, despite all his problems.'

'Maybe people will choose to believe that or maybe they won't, but like I said, it's no concern of mine.'

Tex opened his mouth to respond but then thought better of it and slowly headed down the road towards his hotel. Several people were in the road and Cassidy couldn't help but notice that they avoided looking at him.

For the first time Cassidy felt a twinge of sympathy for him. The news about Katherine being in his hotel all along would already have travelled around town and, from the reactions he'd seen so far, many people viewed his actions in an unfavourable light.

But he turned from watching a man leave who might have destroyed himself because of his love for a woman he couldn't have, to watching another man approach who wouldn't lose a minute's sleep over a woman he could have.

'Explain yourself to McGill then, Emerson?' Cassidy asked when his brother reached him.

'I've got the knack of talking my way out of trouble,' Emerson said, leaning back against the wall beside Cassidy. He wiped mock sweat from his brow.

'And of talking others into trouble.'

'Perhaps.' Emerson glanced to the side to watch Sheriff McGill head out of his office. He didn't speak again until the sheriff had mounted up and was riding out of town. 'But hopefully once he's found Bret and Chalk he can confirm what I told him.'

Cassidy snorted. 'I wouldn't count on them helping you out.'

'I agree, but he's known Bret Sanborn for many years and I reckon he was more inclined to accept my version of events than his.' Emerson watched McGill ride past the last building on the road, then shrugged. 'But either way, I'm leaving before Bret and Chalk can find me.'

Cassidy sighed. 'You still want to get away before you have to see Annie again?'

'Sure do,' Emerson said, blowing out his cheeks for emphasis.

'And what are you so worried about? She's a fine woman.'

'Aren't they all?' Emerson turned to go, but Cassidy shot out a hand, grabbed his collar, and dragged him up close. Emerson considered the hand. 'Don't make the mistake of ordering me to stay, Cassidy.'

'Already have. You see, you've blackened the Yates's good name with your antics here and you'll stay until you've sorted that out.'

'A good man like you can do that.'

Cassidy ignored the sarcasm and tightened his grip.

'I could, but you convinced me you were staying out of loyalty to James's memory. As we still don't know who killed him, your decision to leave means you really were just staying in the hope of getting paid.' Cassidy widened his eyes. 'And that disappoints me.'

Emerson looked at him and his mouth opened as if he was about to blurt out an explanation. Then his gaze rocked to the side.

Cassidy followed his gaze to see that Tex Beatty was loitering in the middle of the road and was looking beyond the edge of town in the opposite direction to the route McGill had taken. Cassidy turned to see what he was looking at and saw the reason for his interest. Six riders were heading into town.

Cassidy didn't recognize five of them, although he knew the look of trouble when he saw it, but he did recognize the leading man.

Luther Manson was riding into town.

11

Nick had yet to finish sweeping out the ash and other debris from the office which Lomax's actions last night had created, when Cassidy kicked open the door and he and Emerson charged inside. Emerson quickly hunkered down beside the window and drew his gun, peering out into the road while Cassidy held the door open. A moment later Tex Beatty thundered inside.

'Everyone keep down,' Cassidy said, looking at each man in the office and gesturing with his palms facing down.

Without a word, Nick hurried behind the linotype machine, the largest cover in the room and ducked down, but he chose a position where he could peer through gaps in the metal casing to see what was happening.

'He's already seen me,' Tex whined, darting his gaze around as he looked for cover.

'I know. That's why you've got to keep your head down and give me a chance of getting you out of this alive.' Cassidy drew his gun. 'And besides, Luther Manson coming here just saves me the trouble of having to track him down.'

Cassidy then gestured for Tex to join Nick in keeping low behind the linotype machine while he and Emerson hunkered down behind Henry's desk at the side of the office, leaving the middle of the office deserted.

Hidden behind the linotype machine, Nick couldn't see what was happening out on the road, but he heard the occasional grunted order and the subdued muttering and clattering of the townsfolk, which suggested everyone was fleeing for cover.

Horses pulled up outside out of view and heavy footfalls approached the office.

Then Luther shouted, his demand coming from the side of the window.

'Come out with the ransom money, Tex Beatty, or die!'

Cassidy bobbed up to look at Tex.

'Tex,' he said, 'why does Luther think he hasn't been paid?'

Tex shrugged and glanced at Nick, but if he was hoping for support, Nick wasn't inclined to give it and he just glared back at him until Tex sighed.

'To tell you the truth,' he said, his low tone suggesting this was in fact the case, 'James's problems near bank-rupted me. I couldn't raise Luther's ransom of five thousand dollars in gold.'

'So what did you do? Pay him in gold-painted bricks?'

'Something like that.' Tex raised his voice. 'Luther Manson, I've got nothing to say to you and nothing more I can give you. So you can — '

A huge crash sounded as a barrel flew through the window, spraying jagged shards of glass around the office.

Cassidy shouted at Nick and Tex to keep down. Nick threw himself to the floor but he'd yet to find the safest position when through the many gaps in the linotype machine he saw the first bandit dare to leap through the broken window.

The man must have been fuelled with manic bravery because Cassidy made him pay for his foolishness with a deadly shot that tore into his chest before he'd even landed on the floor. But then the sheer number of men charging inside forced Cassidy to duck. Two men piled in through the door and the other three leapt in through the window. They sprayed gunfire with such rapidity that Nick joined Tex in pressing himself flat to the floor as lead ricocheted around them. Nick could do nothing but hope that Cassidy and Emerson had been able to dive for safety too.

There was a pause, another brief volley, then a bandit vaulted over the linotype machine to land between them. He landed lightly, gave Nick the shortest of glances, the contemptuous sneer on his scarred face dismissing him as no threat, then spun round to confront Tex.

Tex swung his gun up, but he reacted too slowly and the man kicked his gun hand away, sending the gun spinning to the floor. Then he lunged down and dragged him to his feet.

'I've got him,' he shouted in triumph.

Another cry of delight went up in the office from Luther Manson and Nick heard the pattering of feet closing on him. If he could have burrowed beneath the linotype machine he would have, but he could do nothing but press himself down, making himself as small as possible.

Then a gunshot ripped out. An agonized cry sounded. The linotype machine shook as the running man folded over it, his face lolling down to come to a halt a few inches above Nick's head. He looked up into unseeing eyes and a spot of blood fell and warmed his forehead.

Nick had witnessed many terrible things while he'd attempted to uncover the truth over the last few days, but this was far too shocking for him and he felt something change within him. So far he had chased after a story, but now he realized he'd have to make one for himself if he were to survive. He glanced at the bandit dragging Tex away, then at Tex's gun lying discarded on the floor.

In his whole life Nick had never so much as considered firing a gun, but he'd seen others do it. He steeled himself and when he heard Luther Manson grunt out a taunt to Cassidy, Nick rocked back on his heels, then hurled himself at the gun.

From the corner of his eye he saw the bandit holding Tex turn to follow his progress, then tear his gun away from Tex's neck to shoot him. Tex struggled, redirecting his aim, and Nick heard and felt the whine of a bullet whistle over the back of his neck. Then he closed his grasp around the gun. He drew it back into his hand, cocked it with trembling fingers, then swirled round, leaping to his feet.

He just had time to see that elsewhere in the office Luther Manson and two other bandits were standing in the centre of the office and had Cassidy and Emerson pinned down behind the desk. Both these bandits swirled round to face him, their guns swinging round to shoot him, but Nick blocked that from his mind and concentrated on the one thing he could do. He aimed at the scarred bandit's chest, then fired.

A jolt of pain shot up his arm, knocking Nick backwards, the heavy revolver having a far greater recoil than Nick had thought possible and tumbling him backwards. Three bullets scythed over his tumbling form, only his complete lack of experience with weaponry saving him from the bandits' gunfire.

He hit the floor flat on his back, but he kept the gun in hand and despite the numbness in his wrist and fingers he swung the gun back towards his previous target. He saw that the bandit who had been holding Tex was lying holed and sprawled and Tex was wrestling himself free. And even better, Cassidy and Emerson bobbed up and each of them made one of the remaining bandits pay for firing at him with shots to the side that wheeled them to the floor.

This just left Luther Manson. With a roar of pure rage Luther ignored everything but getting Nick. He vaulted over the linotype machine, landed on the other side, then ripped his gun up. Nick reacted, swinging his gun round to aim at Luther in a futile attempt that he knew he'd never finish. Long before his gun centred on its target a gunshot peeled out.

Nick winced, steeling himself for the worst, but then saw a flash of pain contort Luther's features. He took a stumbling pace towards Nick, dropped to his knees, then keeled over to land face down, his gun clattering away from his slack fingers.

Then there was nothing left to do but for Cassidy and Emerson to emerge from behind the desk and check that they'd taken care of all of the bandits.

'You saved my life,' Tex said, coming over to Nick. He held out his hand to drag him to his feet.

Nick ran his shocked gaze over the dead bandits, shivered, then forced himself to move, but he climbed to his feet without Tex's help.

'Just because I don't like you, it doesn't mean I'd let Luther Manson kill you.'

As Tex struggled for words, Cassidy grunted his agreement.

'With that attitude, Nick,' he said, 'if you decide not to be a newspaper man, I reckon you'll make a fine lawman.'

'That attitude does do you credit,' Tex said, finding his voice at last. 'So despite the contempt you feel for me, I still hope you'll reconsider staying here.'

'I can't,' Nick said. He laid a hand on

the linotype machine that Henry would never teach him how to operate and bade the life he could have had here good-bye. 'I just don't like your terms.'

★ ★ ★

'Enjoy your whiskey,' Emerson said, setting the two glasses and a bottle down on the table, then sitting down.

Cassidy poured two measures, then fingered his glass, now starting to relax. It'd been two hours since he'd dealt with Luther Manson and although the approaching evening gave him plenty of reasons to return to Monotony, he'd remained to ensure that the only outstanding matter that concerned him was in fact over. So he'd kicked his heels waiting for Sheriff McGill to return so that he could relate the details of Luther's demise to him. And, he hoped, receive confirmation that Emerson was no longer a suspect in the search for James Glover's killer. While he waited for him, he had agreed to share a drink with his brother in the saloon.

'You know,' he said, nodding to the bottle, 'this is the first whiskey bottle we've shared in a saloon.'

'It is,' Emerson said, smiling as he took his glass.

'But that's only because you left town before — '

'Cassidy,' Emerson said, raising a hand, 'that's enough about what happened ten years ago.'

'Hard not to do that when we've shared so little else.' Cassidy glared at Emerson a while, but then softened his expression and in deference to Emerson's request, he avoided mentioning the one thing they had shared ten years ago.

'Then just enjoy this whiskey with your elder brother, and if I enjoy it too, I might feel inclined to stop over in Monotony once in a while and have another drink with my younger brother.'

Cassidy sipped his drink. 'I'd prefer to think I might stop over in Eagle

Heights once in a while and spend some time with you instead.'

Emerson winced. 'That's not going to happen. I'm moving on before Bret and Chalk track me down.'

'Sheriff McGill should be able to solve that problem. I believe him to be a persuasive lawman.'

'He might, but I'm not taking the risk.'

Cassidy opened his mouth to argue some more but then sighed and nodded towards the door.

'I don't reckon you've got much choice no more,' he murmured as he considered the two men who were pushing through the batwings. The darkening sky was behind them. The light from inside highlighted the harsh lines of their drawn and determined faces. 'Bret and Chalk are here.'

Emerson tensed but kept his back to the door.

'They seen me?'

'Yup. And from the thunderous look on Chalk's face, Sheriff McGill either hasn't seen them yet or he did nothing to appease them.'

'Emerson Yates!' Chalk shouted from the door. 'Get your ugly hide out of that chair. You and I have got to sort this out once and for all.'

Emerson stayed looking at Cassidy for long enough to urge him to stay out of this with a shake of the head, then stood. He turned to face Chalk, leaving Cassidy sitting.

Emerson considered Chalk's stance, his hand dangling close to his holster, then watched him pace sideways into the saloon. Bret also nudged into the saloon but paced away in the opposite direction to leave Emerson, Chalk and him standing broadly in a triangle.

'You seen Sheriff McGill,' Emerson said, 'and heard his opinion?'

'Nope. Annie sent us off looking for you down by the river, but we figured out where you'd gone for ourselves. Now we've got no reason to avoid this no more.'

Emerson shrugged. 'There's no need

to end this with you all full of holes.'

The taunt made Chalk smile as he welcomed Emerson's decision to take him on.

'Only person dying here is you.'

'Tell that to Luther Manson's gang. I helped Cassidy see them off and so the likes of you are sure not going to worry me.'

A momentary flash of concern clouded Chalk's eyes, but Emerson's comment was so demeaning it only went to strengthen his determination.

'I reckon I'll take that chance.' Chalk set his feet wide, causing a general drifting away from his line of fire throughout the saloon, although Cassidy stayed sitting where he was. 'Go for your gun or I'll shoot you where you stand.'

'And,' Bret said from Emerson's side, 'if you do go for that gun, I'll make sure you die whether you kill Chalk or not.'

Emerson darted his gaze between the two men, while Cassidy scraped back his chair a mite, drawing Bret's and Chalk's attention to him.

'You're both forgetting about me,' he said. 'I've got me a gun drawn under this table and it's making sure neither of you carry out those threats.'

'Stay out this, Cassidy,' Bret said. 'This is between us and Emerson.'

'I can well understand why you're so annoyed, seeing as how you reckon Emerson has mistreated your daughter, but you've got to ask yourself why Chalk is so determined to kill him.'

'For the same reason.'

'I don't reckon so.' Cassidy fixed his gaze on Chalk, looking for his reaction. 'I know you were all set to build that home for you and Annie down by the river where that old shack is, but now you can't do that no more.'

'Because of Emerson,' Chalk grunted.

'That wasn't the reason. The chance had already gone before Emerson came along. James Glover lent you the money to build that home, but then he wanted the money back to repay his debts. And I'm guessing he added on plenty of interest, and I'm also guessing you couldn't repay him and so had no choice but to leave it as a shack. And I find it mighty odd that Jackson Dyer, the man who identified Katherine Glover to Luther Manson, just happened to rest up in that shack. Almost makes me wonder whether you hired him.'

From the corner of his eye he saw Bret flinch, then turn his gaze away from Emerson to look at Chalk.

'Is this true?' he asked.

Chalk gulped. 'This ain't got nothing to do with nothing.'

'But it has,' Cassidy said. 'You've been determined to kill Emerson far beyond the point that any reasonable man would carry on a grievance — and believe me I know how any man in your position should feel. And you did that, not because of Annie, not because you reckon Emerson killed James Glover, but because a dead man can't explain that he didn't kill James. And that would let you cover up your actions and your real motive of ensuring nobody could work out who did kill him.'

The accusation hung in the air unanswered and in truth Cassidy had nothing to back up the allegation other than a hunch and the conviction in his gaze as he glared at Chalk.

But that conviction was enough and with a great roar of defiance Chalk threw his hand to his gun. He never got to draw it. Cassidy blasted lead up through the table from his drawn gun. More gunshots blasted and echoed in the saloon as Chalk stumbled backwards into the wall, his chest holed.

And as he slid to the floor, Cassidy noted that beside the hole in his chest that he'd made, there were two other bullet holes from two other guns.

Cassidy then turned his gun on Bret, but the fight had now gone out of Bret. He holstered his gun and turned to go, his shoulders slumped and defeated by his decision to back the wrong man.

'This has ended it, hasn't it?' Cassidy said to him.

'Yeah,' Bret murmured, not looking

back but stopping long enough to sneer at Emerson, 'so long as you stay away from my daughter.'

Emerson raised his hands high with a resigned gesture that said he had no problem in complying with that demand, but Cassidy grunted his irritation.

'That matter is between Annie and Emerson.'

'It ain't.' Bret walked towards the door. 'I only let suitable men come anywhere near her.'

Cassidy watched him deliberately give Chalk's body a contemptuous wide berth and he waited until he had a hand on the batwings before he spoke again.

'How can you trust your judgement on who is suitable for your daughter when the man you approved of is lying there all full of holes?'

Bret looked into the road, unable to find a response. Without further word he nudged the batwings apart and disappeared from view.

Emerson watched him go then turned to Cassidy.

'You had no need to fight for me over her,' he said.

'But I reckon I had,' Cassidy said, standing. He looked out through the saloon window, then moved to the side so that he could see the half-moon that was now lighting the evening sky. He beckoned Emerson to follow him out. 'And I reckon after everything you've done to me and all the help I've given you, that you owe me a favour before you go.'

12

Nick looked down the tracks.

The next train wouldn't arrive for another week but he figured he'd spend that time waiting here at the station. Then, as he had been successful when he'd worked as a train butch, he could return to doing that again while he waited for another chance to do the work that he now viewed as being his calling.

He heard footsteps and turned. He wasn't surprised to see Tex Beatty approaching.

'I've got nothing to say to you,' Nick said, turning back to look at the tracks.

'But I'd hoped you might have reconsidered now you've had time to think things through. Not only did Cassidy Yates get Luther Manson, he also worked out who killed James Glover. News of that magnitude ought to be read about in the Eagle Heights *Chronicle*.'

Nick had to admit he wished he could write up the report that explained how all those matters linked up, but he folded his arms and kept his chin high.

'I'd heard, but get someone else to report on it.'

Tex sighed, and when he spoke it was with greater honesty in his tone than Nick had heard before.

'What can I say to make you reconsider?'

'Nothing,' Nick said, hardening his mind to any reasonable offer. 'Like I said — I don't like your terms.'

'Then don't have any terms. The *Chronicle* office and everything in it is yours.'

Nick gulped, his heart actually feeling as if it'd skipped a beat. He had expected Tex to make him an offer, but never one of this magnitude, and he couldn't help but turn and stare at Tex aghast until he regained his composure with a firm shake of the head.

'That is a trap so many others have fallen into before and I won't be in your pay.'

'I never said you would be. I was doing it out of gratitude, and because you remind me of a young Henry Sinclair.'

A voice in his mind was clamouring at Nick to accept, but still he resisted the urge and he moved to head by Tex and find a different place to stand on the platform.

'I don't believe you know what gratitude is, and Henry stood for printing the truth. If I'm in your debt, I can never do that.'

'You're not in my debt. I'm giving you the newspaper. You're free to print the truth, no matter whom that may hurt. And that includes me because . . . because maybe sometimes I need to hear it.' He uttered a single snorting laugh. 'After all, the people in my pay sure won't pay me the kindness of doing that, and it might alert me to what people like Lomax are doing in my name.'

Nick looked at the tracks then at the station, imagining the long wait for a train that faced him.

'I suppose,' he mused, 'I could try this for a week and see how it goes.'

'You could.' Tex laughed then even gave Nick a slap on the back. 'That's just what Henry Sinclair said fifteen years ago, and if he was here now, you know what he'd say?'

Nick raised his eyebrows. 'What?'

'That news is only news while someone will pay to read it. You've got a report to get out and while you're considering my offer, you're just wasting your time and your money.'

This was something Nick could agree on and already he could envisage the report he would write . . .

He shook that appealing thought away and stood tall.

'Remember this — I will run the *Chronicle* my way and print my stories my way.' Nick glared at Tex, but then sighed and spread his hands. 'But I will only ever print the truth.'

'Nobody could ask for anything more,' Tex said.

'Then stop wasting my time talking to me. I've got a special issue of the Eagle Heights *Chronicle* to get out.' Nick couldn't help but smile as he walked past Tex. 'And this one might run to four pages, at four times the price.'

* * *

With the moon at their backs, Cassidy and Emerson stood at the top of the Devil's Ridge. Down below them was the ranch.

'This is pointless, Cassidy,' Emerson said. 'Nothing you can say will make me go down there. I just ain't that sort of man.'

'Every man is that sort of man. Tex made plenty of mistakes because of Katherine, and Chalk made plenty of mistakes because of Annie, and . . . and I guess I've done it before too. But the important thing is to realize they're mistakes then make the right decision about your future.'

Emerson snorted. 'I don't need no lectures about women from my younger brother.'

'And I think you do. You're impatient, always eager to move on, but I don't see what you gain when you do. You just move on into a different town and make all the same mistakes again. Perhaps if you stayed in one place you might not make so many mistakes.'

'That's something I don't intend to find out.' Emerson turned to go. 'It was a good try, Cassidy, but I've listened to you like I promised to and now I'm going.'

'Then before you go, tell me one thing. What are you so scared of down there?'

Emerson turned. 'I'm not scared of Bret. I can see him off, no trouble, no trouble at all.'

Cassidy forced out a snorting laugh. 'Seeing off your woman's father might not be the best idea any man ever had.'

'I wouldn't need to fight him. I could talk him round if I wanted to.'

'I'm sure you could, but I'm talking about Annie. What are you scared of with her? You keep on moving on, looking for novelty you can't find, but why not try the greatest novelty of all — making something work with one woman in one place.'

'Doesn't sound like a novelty to me,' Emerson grumbled.

Cassidy smiled as he detected a change in Emerson's tone and he leaned forward.

'How can you say that if you haven't tried it before?' He shrugged. 'Give it a year, six months, and if it don't work out, move on when you've exhausted all the novelty of staying in one place.'

Emerson sighed. 'You won't stop badgering me until I give in, will you?'

'Nope,' Cassidy said with some relish as he realized Emerson was letting him talk him round to his way of thinking.

Emerson looked down at the ranch where, with impeccable timing that

Cassidy couldn't have arranged even if he'd tried, a light came on in Annie's window.

'Three months, you say?' Emerson asked as the light came and went twice more.

Cassidy was about to correct him, but as he reckoned that before that time was over, Annie would be sure to give him news that would either drive him away or keep him, he nodded.

'Three months it is. And then I'll be back to see you.'

'Why?'

Cassidy shrugged. 'Because you're kin and it'd sure be nice to visit a family.'

'Family?' Emerson murmured as if he'd never uttered that word before, but his bewildered tone didn't suggest he'd gathered Cassidy's other meaning. 'Yeah, a visit would be fine.'

Then there was nothing left for the two men to say or do but to nod to each other, shake hands and finally, in a brief self-conscious gesture, give each other a back-slapping hug.

Then Emerson set off down to the ranch.

As he watched his brother leave, Cassidy wished him well. He couldn't say with any assurance that Emerson would be able to bring himself to stay with Annie, but he hoped he would.

Either way, he had achieved what he'd set out to do. Emerson was riding down from Devil's Ridge with the moon at his back to return to Annie. The rest was up to Emerson and to Annie.

And that was good enough for Cassidy.

THE END

Other titles in the
Linford Western Library:

FIND MADIGAN!

Hank J. Kirby

Bronco Madigan was the top man in the US Marshals' Service — and now he was missing. Working on the most important and most dangerous mission he'd ever been assigned, he'd disappeared into the gunsmoke. Everything pointed to him being one of the many dead bodies left along the bloody trail. Even his sidekick, Kimble, was almost ready to give up the search, but the Chief's orders were very clear: 'Find Madigan . . . at all costs!'

MISFIT LIL GETS EVEN

Chap O'Keefe

While Silver Vein's citizens watch 'Misfit Lil' shine in a gala shooting match, Yuma Nat Hawkins and his gang rob the bank and gun down the depleted opposition in cold blood. Patrick 'Preacher' Kilkieran witnesses the robbery, but keeps his distance — and is soon striking a mysterious deal with a renegade Indian before fleeing town. But it's Kilkieran's brutal assault on Lil's friend Estelle that compels her to vow retribution and track him down . . .

ON THE WAPITI RANGE

Owen G. Irons

When wapiti hunters arrive on Lee Trent's Green River preserve, they bring trouble by carrying too many guns into his peaceful realm. If that weren't enough, they are also holding prisoner a beautiful madwoman in a windowless wagon. The elk hunters' presence threatens to bring Lee into conflict with the Cheyenne Indians, and his neighbours. Then disaster follows when the hunt becomes a slaughter. And Lee must handle the invaders by himself if he is to recover his mountain domain.

ARIZONA SHOWDOWN

Corba Sunman

Travis Jordan was a bounty hunter with his own reasons for turning his back on normal life. Then someone appeared from his past with a plea for help. Family duty reached for him, which he could not ignore, and he returned to his home range. But once he drew his pistol, he would be unable to holster it until the last shot in a bitter clean-up had been fired. It was kill-or-be-killed — and he was resolute that he would win . . .

HILLS OF BLOOD

Frank Weight

To the Confederate prisoners of the
Civil War the offer seemed almost
too good to be true: volunteer to
fight the Indians and receive free-
dom in return. Captain Terrance saw
the chance to escape the living hell
of the prison and ordered his men to
enlist in the special corps. Now he
has the opportunity to look for the
fabulous gold of the Red Hills
— and to strike a blow for the South
in the war which, to him, is
all-important . . .